ISABEL LEICESTER

A ROMANCE

CLOTILDA JENNINGS

1st WORLD
LIBRARY
Literary Society

Isabel Leicester

Clotilda Jennings

© 1st World Library, 2007
PO Box 2211
Fairfield, IA 52556
www.1stworldlibrary.com
First Edition

LCCN: 2007927846

Softcover ISBN: 978-1-4218-4517-3
Hardcover ISBN: 978-1-4218-4433-6
eBook ISBN: 978-1-4218-4601-9

Purchase *"Isabel Leicester"*
as a traditional bound book at:
www.1stWorldLibrary.com/purchase.asp?ISBN=978-1-4218-4517-3

1st World Library is a literary, educational organization
dedicated to:

- Creating a free internet library of downloadable ebooks

- Hosting writing competitions and offering book publishing
  scholarships.

Interested in more 1st World Library books? contact:
literacy@1stworldlibrary.com
Check us out at: www.1stworldlibrary.com

1ˢᵗ World Library Literary Society

Giving Back to the World

"If you want to work on the core problem, it's early school literacy."

- **James Barksdale, former CEO of Netscape**

"No skill is more crucial to the future of a child, or to a democratic and prosperous society, than literacy."

- **Los Angeles Times**

"Literacy... means far more than learning how to read and write... The aim is to transmit... knowledge and promote social participation."

- **UNESCO**

"Literacy is not a luxury, it is a right and a responsibility. If our world is to meet the challenges of the twenty-first century we must harness the energy and creativity of all our citizens."

- **President Bill Clinton**

"Parents should be encouraged to read to their children, and teachers should be equipped with all available techniques for teaching literacy, so the varying needs and capacities of individual kids can be taken into account."

- **Hugh Mackay**

"Twist ye, twine ye, even so,
Mingled threads of joy and woe,
Hope and fear, peace and strife,
In the cord of human life."

HAMILTON:
SPECTATOR PRINTING HOUSE.
1874.

CHAPTER I

In a spacious apartment superbly furnished, and surrounded by every luxury that could please the most fastidious taste, sat Isabel Leicester, attired in deep mourning, with her head resting upon her hand, her face almost as white as the handkerchief she held. Isabel's Father had failed in business, and the misfortune had so preyed upon his mind, that he sank under it and died. The funeral had taken place that day, and she was to leave the house on the day following—the house where she was born and had always lived, except when at school. The servants had all been discharged but two, who were to leave next day. A friend had offered Isabel a home until she could procure a situation as a governess, which that friend Mrs. Arnold was endeavouring to obtain for her, in the family of a lady who had been one of Mrs. Arnold's school-fellows. Mrs. Arnold was the widow of a clergyman, with a very limited income, and Isabel was unwilling to trespass upon the kindness of one whose means she knew to be so small. But she had no alternative at the time and trusted that it would not be long before she would be able to procure the situation she had in view, or some other. The tea remained untasted on the table, for Isabel was absorbed by the melancholy thoughts that filled her heart. She tried to feel resigned, but her pride was wounded at the idea of becoming a 'governess.' She had been the spoiled petted daughter of a wealthy merchant of the city of New York, whose chief delight had been to indulge her in every way. But still Mr. Leicester had been a truly good and christian man, and had taught his daughter not to set her affections on earthly things, and to remember that wealth was given to us for the benefit of others, as well as for our own enjoyment. And he was rewarded as she grew up to find that her chief aim was to do good to the many poor families whose necessities came to her knowledge. Great also was his satisfaction to find that after two seasons in New York, where she had been the Belle, she was still the same loving, unassuming, pure-minded girl she had ever been, tho' the admiration and attention her beauty and accomplishments had excited, had she been less carefully trained, might have rendered her haughty and vain.

During her Father's illness, when her time and thoughts were occupied with attending upon him, and in anxiety for his recovery she had thought and felt that the loss of property was an evil of little moment, and tried to persuade her Father not to think so much about the reverse, urging that he could get some employment, and they would still live very happily together in a cottage.

But now that he was gone, and she had no one left to look too, her lonely and self-dependant position was felt severely, and the tears she could not restrain, fell unheeded. The fire sank low, and finally went out, and still Isabel sat thinking of the miserable prospect the future presented. At last she rose with a shudder, and rang for the tea-things to be removed, then retiring to her own room, she threw herself upon the bed in an agony of grief.

She had remained there some time, when she felt a kind hand laid upon her shoulder, and turning her head she saw the old housekeeper, Mrs. Stewart, with a cup of hot tea. "Come my dear young lady," said she, while the tears streamed down

Clotilda Jennings

her aged cheeks, "You must take this, it will never do for you to go without your tea."

"I know you attach great virtue to a cup of tea" replied Isabel, "so to please you I will take it."

"Oh dear, dear," muttered the old woman as she descended the stairs, "how pale and ill she looks, and no wonder poor lamb, if she goes on like this she will be laid up. Oh, how I wish Mrs. Mornington had not gone to Europe. Poor child, poor child."

After Mrs. Stewart had left her, Isabel knelt down and prayed for strength to do her duty, however trying she might find it, and for the holy spirit to comfort her in affliction, after which she retired to rest, and was soon in a calm sleep.

Next morning she arose much refreshed, and having sought divine aid and protection, she commenced to arrange for her departure. Her Father's creditors knowing him to be a man of strict integrity, and that his failure was not attributable to any want of prudence on his part, had kindly arranged that she should retain whatever she particularly wished. This was a great gratification to Isabel, tho' she was too honorable to take an undue advantage of this benevolent intention, indeed she was almost too conscientious upon this point.

The task before her was a sad one, and although she strove very hard she could not restrain her tears as she made her selections. She was soon joined by Mrs. Arnold, who told her she had come to help her to pack, and that she should not leave until Isabel accompanied her. "Come" she said, kissing her affectionately, "the sooner this painful task is over my love the better. I have good news for you. I have heard from Mrs. Arlington, and she says that she shall be most happy to obtain the services of any one recommended by me. The salary I find is only two hundred dollars a year, it is indeed less than I expected, but you must remember that this is your first engagement, no doubt if you remain there a year or two, you will be able to obtain a much more remunerative one."

This announcement of Mrs. Arnold's brought to Isabel's mind in full force all the annoyances to which she would be subjected in her new position, and clasping her hands, she gave way to uncontrollable emotion.

"I do not wonder, dear, at your being disappointed, after what you have been used to, two hundred dollars must seem a very paltry sum. I dare say you gave nearly as much to your maid Harris, but my dear, as a governess your requirements will be less, so with the wardrobe you now possess, you will be able to manage very nicely."

"Oh, Mrs. Arnold, I was not thinking about the salary, I am sure I can make that do very well," sobbed Isabel. "You are very kind indeed to trouble yourself so much about me."

"You need not go to Elm Grove at present, my love, you are quite welcome to stay with me until you get over your loss a little, and feel better able to conform to circumstances," said Mrs. Arnold kindly.

Isabel made an effort to respond gratefully to her kind friend, and expressed a hope that she would shortly be able to undertake the duties of her new situation.

"I have no doubt you will be very comfortable at Elm Grove, it is a lovely place. Of course it will seem strange at first, but people soon get used to a place you know if they only try. I am very happy now, but I am sure at one time, I thought I never should be again," continued Mrs. Arnold, "but we will say no more on that subject now, we must get on with our work." And she began to give advice about what Isabel should take, and said that whatever she did not like to take with her to her new home, she could leave at her house.

Fortunately the housekeeper then came to ask if she should pack.

"Certainly," exclaimed Mrs. Arnold, "the very person I wanted," and off they went to Isabel's great relief.

Being left to herself, Isabel soon concluded her selection, and ordering Mary to take them to be packed, she went into the library to get a little rest, and time to think, tho' the latter she could scarcely do, as her temples throbbed violently. Laying her head on the old familiar couch, she endeavoured to calm the tumult of her feelings, the bright sunshine, and the merry sound of the sleigh bells outside, only made her feel her desolation more acutely.

"Luncheon is ready dear, and the packing all done," said Mrs. Arnold, throwing herself in an easy chair.

"You have indeed been quick," replied Isabel, heartily wishing they had been longer.

"It is all due to Mrs. Stewart, she is really the most clever person at packing I ever saw, tho' poor soul she was nearly blinded with tears. Come love, we must have luncheon now, and after that we will send for a sleigh."

"Indeed, dear Mrs. Arnold, I cannot go until evening, I am sure Mr. Macdermott will be here presently, for he knows that I am going to-day."

"Ah, I know, you want to be alone to muse of things in your dreamy way, but my love, it is better not to do so, it only makes things harder to bear. Try to banish disagreeable subjects as much as possible, that is my maxim. But I cannot refuse you anything just now, so after luncheon I will go home, and will come back for you in the evening."

Soon after Mrs. Arnold's departure, Mr. Macdermott the clergyman, called as Isabel had expected, and his sympathy, and advice, tended greatly to soothe the pain she felt at leaving the home she loved so well. He said that Mrs. Macdermott was still too ill to visit her, but that if she felt able she would try to see her at Mrs. Arnold's. He told her also that he had that morning received a letter from Louis, in which he desired to be kindly remembered. Mr. Macdermott remarked the rich crimson that suffused her cheeks, at the mention of his nephew's name, but the remotest idea of their engagement never entered his mind. He remained with her about an hour, then after enquiring if he could be of any service to her, he took his leave.

At last the dreaded hour arrived, and Mrs. Arnold with it. After bidding the housekeeper and Mary a kind farewell, (they had both been with her a great many years,) Isabel accompanied her friend to Rose Cottage.

CHAPTER II

The setting sun shed its bright tints over the snow which lay thick upon the ground, making it glisten like diamonds, the cold was intense, and a bitter wind howled through the leafless trees, when the train arrived at M—, and Isabel almost benumbed with cold, procured a conveyance from the station to the Rock Hotel, where Mrs. Arlington had promised to send for her.

On arriving at the hotel, she found the sleigh waiting punctual to the time appointed. Isabel would gladly have partaken of some refreshment, but Mrs. Arnold had informed her, that Mrs. Arlington was very particular, and to have kept the horses standing, Isabel felt would have offended her, which she was very anxious to avoid although she was shivering with cold.

It was a long drive of twelve miles to Elm Grove, but the horses went at a great speed, and in less than an hour they arrived at their destination. As they drew up at the door, it was opened by a footman, and a woman who seemed to be an upper servant met her in the hall, and conducted her to her room.

"I suppose you would like some tea Miss," she said "I will order it while you are taking off your things, and then I will show you the school-room. Mrs. Arlington and the young ladies are dressing for a ball, so they cannot see you to-night."

When Norris had left the room, Isabel sat down with a sigh, and looked about to see what kind of accommodation she was to have. It was a nice sized room, with a bay window having an eastern aspect, at which the wind was now howling with great violence. It was neatly, but plainly furnished, the fire had burnt low, and the room was cold. She took off her things as quickly as possible, and sincerely hoped that the school-room would be more comfortable.

Norris soon returned, and Isabel desiring her to have more fuel put upon the fire descended to the school-room, which she found very bright and pleasant looking, the large fire and lamp making it look quite attractive.

The tea was on the table, and Norris after saying "if you want anything Miss, please ring for Susan," left the room. Isabel was very glad to have some refreshment after her cold drive, and when she rang to have the things removed, the bell was answered by a neat, pleasant looking girl, who had such a sunny face that it did one good to look at her, and presently a sweet little girl of about seven years old came running into the room, and going up to Isabel, said "you are our new governess are you not. I think I shall like you very much, but I can't stay now, for Eliza is waiting to put me to bed, but I did so want to see you to-night. Good night!" and throwing her arms round Isabel's neck, she gave her a hearty kiss, and disappeared as quickly as she came. When Isabel returned to her room she had no cause to complain of the fire which was piled to the top of the grate.

When she awoke next morning it seemed very strange to be where she had not the least idea what any of the family were like. After dressing and arranging some of her things, she sat down to contemplate her situation, which she found anything but pleasant, so she determined to descend to the school-room.

The door was open, and as she approached she overheard little Amy saying "she is the prettiest lady I ever saw, only she looks so pale and sad." Isabel found three little girls in the room, of whom Amy was the youngest. Amy greeted her in the same cordial manner she had done on the preceding evening, the other two rose saying "good morning Miss Leicester," but when she stooped to kiss them, Alice sulkily put up her face, and Rose laughed. "Fancy, Miss Manning kissing us" she whispered to her sister. "Hush!" returned Alice, "she will hear."

Isabel spoke kindly to them, but Alice only returned unwilling, and Rose pert answers, so the breakfast was a dull unpleasant affair, and Isabel perceived they regarded the governess in the light of an enemy; even little Amy became shy and uneasy.

After breakfast Rose informed her that they always had half an hour before school for a run out of doors. As they were departing little Amy ran back, and coming close up to Isabel whispered "don't cry Miss Leicester, I love you, indeed I do," for Amy had noticed the tears that would come in spite of her efforts to repress them. Isabel drew the child to her, and kissing her pretty upturned face, told her to go with the others.

Amy had scarcely gone, when Mrs. Arlington entered. She was tall and stately, rather cold and haughty, and very digni-fied and patronizing in her manner. She hoped Miss Leicester had been made comfortable, and was sure that she would like the children. She then informed her that the school hours were from nine until four, with an hour for dinner, then she would have to take them for a walk, after that her time was her own. She would take her meals with the children, but she would be happy to have her come into the drawing-room occasionally in the evening. She said that her own time was so much occupied with her elder daughters, that she was forced to leave the children entirely to the governess, but, that as Mrs. Arnold had so strongly recommended her she felt sure she should be satisfied, then bidding Miss Leicester a polite good morning, she swept majestically from the room.

Poor Isabel, she had not expected quite so much dignity, and was excessively annoyed. "Take the children for walks," that was a thing she had not thought of, and she did not relish the idea and as to going into the drawing-room, she could very well dispense with that. She was not aware that Mrs. Arlington intended her accomplished young governess to help to amuse her guests. Excessively annoyed, Isabel repaired to her own room to calm her ruffled feelings.

At nine o'clock she went to the school-room and found her pupils there already, also a very pretty girl of about seventeen, whom they were coaxing to tell them about the ball. As Isabel entered the room, Amy exclaimed, "Miss Leicester this is Emily!" Then Emily laughed merrily, and held out her hand saying, "I hope we shall be good friends Miss Leicester, I'm sorry we were out last night."

"Oh! Emily, I'm sure you wanted very much to go to the ball, and you just now said that you enjoyed yourself exceedingly," said Alice gravely.

"I didn't mean that you silly child, returned Emily, but I am intruding upon school hours I fear, so if you will allow me Miss Leicester I will come for a chat before dinner."

Isabel bowed assent and Emily retired, rather annoyed that her advances had not met with a warmer reception. Shortly after Emily's departure, a tall and very elegant looking girl of about twenty entered the room, and bowing condescendingly to Isabel, said, "have the goodness to try these songs Miss Leicester, I wish to know if there are any pretty ones among them, I would not trouble you only I am so excessively tired" she added, taking the most comfortable seat the room afforded; this was done in the most easy manner possible, precluding of course the idea that it was by design. Miss Arlington upon entering any room, immediately perceived the nicest place, and having seen, at once took possession with an easy indifference, as if totally unconscious that she was monopolizing the best place. Isabel complied with her request, tho' not best pleased with the interruption.

"You sing very nicely Miss Leicester," Miss Arlington said patronizingly.

Isabel's lip curled contemptuously, she presumed so when the crowded room had been hushed to perfect silence whenever she approached the piano, and when she ceased singing, the murmured praise and applause on all sides had sent the hot blood to her cheeks, and this not once or twice, but scores of times—she needed not to be told that she sang nicely.

"She sings much better than you do Grace," said Rose pertly.

"Don't be rude, Rose," replied Grace, haughtily, "Miss Leicester will have some trouble with you I imagine," then thanking Isabel, she left the room excessively annoyed with Rose.

The lessons proceeded, and Isabel thought that Alice and Rose must alter their manners greatly before she could take any interest in teaching them. It was evident that they had not been treated kindly by their last governess. Alice sulked so much, and Rose was so pert, that Isabel found it difficult to keep her temper, and when tea was over, her head ached so severely, and she felt so tired and miserable, that she retired to her room, and locking herself in gave way to irrepressible emotion, while she thought that she should indeed be unhappy in her new position.

Presently some one knocked at the door, but vexed at the interruption, and not wishing to be seen giving way to her feelings, Isabel took no notice. As the knocking continued unanswered, a soft voice pleaded for admittance. On opening the door, she found it was Emily, and not Amy, as she expected.

"I hope you will excuse me," she said, "but not finding you in the school-room I came after you, as I knew that I should not have any other opportunity this evening."

Isabel was very much confused, but Emily sat down by her side, telling her how very much she felt for her, and how she hoped she would consider her a friend. "Mrs. Arnold wrote and told me all about you" she said, "and dear Isabel I will do all in my power to make you happy."

But Isabel only sobbed, "I can never be happy again— never."

"You must not say that, you must not think so," exclaimed Emily. "You must come into the drawing-room with us, and that will cheer you up a bit. I know you will like papa. Elm Grove looks dreary now, but in summer it is delightful. Then, I always get up early and go for a ramble before breakfast, if I can only get any one to go with me, and I feel sure you will go with me next summer. I think I shall breakfast with you, I can't wait for mama's late breakfast, but I would sooner have gone without altogether, than have taken it with Miss Manning. I only left school you know a few weeks ago, and I like a little fun. I know I make the children very outrageous sometimes, but then, you know I could not behave at all like a fashionable young lady in the evening, if I did not get rid of some of my wild spirits before hand. By-the-bye," she cried, laughing, "I believe you will have to teach me manners, Miss Massie pronounced me quite incorrigible, my sister is a perfect model according to her idea, but I could never be like Grace, I think mamma has given up all thought of it."

"I don't know about teaching you manners, but I must try what I can do with Alice and Rose, they are sadly deficient even in politeness."

"Ah, you have found that out already have you," cried Emily laughing.

Isabel colored, and murmured something about forgetting who she was speaking to. "O you needn't mind, I like people who say what they think" said Emily, "besides that is just what papa says about them, but you must own that Amy is a nice little thing, I don't think she could be rude or unkind."

"Yes Amy is a sweet child."

"It will not be quite so dull here next week, for Everard is coming home. I do wish so much for you to see him, he is my idea of perfection as far as attainable in human nature. Oh! he's so handsome, and such a dear nice fellow, I'm sure you will like him."

"Perhaps you are not an impartial judge, I may not be able to see his perfections so clearly."

"You can't help seeing them, they are as clear as daylight," returned Emily, warmly. "What do you think he asked me in his last letter—to tell him what sort of a gorgon the new governess was, so as I wrote to-day, I said she was beyond all description, and not to be compared with Miss Manning, so if he does not imagine something awful its very strange, (Isabel did not look well pleased) I hope you wont mind; it was such a nice opportunity for a trick, but it is time I dressed for dinner, dear me how tiresome, and away she bounded. What a funny girl, thought Isabel, I wonder if I shall like her, at all events she means to be kind.

CHAPTER III

Isabel was not happy in her new home, it was no easy task to teach such unruly girls as Alice and Rose, whose chief object was to get as much fun as possible at the expense of their governess, but she trusted in time to be able to bring them to better order by the exercise of firmness and kindness combined. With Amy, however it was quite different, she seemed never so happy as when with Isabel.

It was Sunday afternoon, the children did not seem to know how to employ themselves, but sat sullenly each with a book, tho' it was very evident that they were not reading. Indeed, Isabel had seen by their manners all day, that they had not been accustomed to have Sunday made pleasant.

"Come here Amy dear," said Isabel, "would you like me to read to you."

"Yes please, for it makes my head ache to read all the afternoon."

So Isabel read a portion of scripture and several nice little hymns. Very soon as she had expected, Alice and Rose, drew near. Then she read them part of the 'chief's daughter,' and after that she played several sacred pieces and sang a hymn to the tune tranquility. The children all gathered round her asking her to teach them to sing it. She promised to do so if they would learn the words, which they immediately commenced to do.

After tea they had a most unexpected and very welcome visitor. "Oh! Everard, when did you come home," they all exclaimed.

"While you were at church," he returned.

"What a shame you didn't come to see us before," said Alice reproachfully.

"O then, I suppose it was you who shut the door when we were singing this afternoon," interposed Rose, "why didn't you come in."

"I did not wish to disturb you" he answered, "but why don't some of you have the politeness to introduce me to your new governess."

Isabel colored deeply as he used the distasteful appellation, and bent lower over her book, and when Rose said, Mr. Everard Arlington, Miss Leicester," her bow was more haughty and dignified than she was aware of. He seated himself at the window with Amy on his knee, while the others stood one on either side. Isabel heard a great deal being said about Miss Leicester in an under tone, and was about to leave the room, when Everard interposed, saying "I shall go, unless you stay Miss Leicester, I'm not going to turn you out of the room."

"Indeed I would rather go," said Isabel.

"Indeed I would rather you stayed." returned Everard.

Clotilda Jennings

"I do not wish to be any restraint on the children, it would be better for me to go."

"Well," said Everard putting his hand on the door, "I may as well have it out with you at once, as I did with Miss Manning, I am very fond of my little sisters, and often come to see them here."

"I have no objection, only let me go."

"But that is just what I don't want you to do, and I always have my own way at Elm Grove. You must not run away whenever I come, or I shall think you consider me an intruder."

"Never mind what I think," said Isabel looking up, about to insist upon going, for she was very indignant at his behaviour, but the face she beheld quite disarmed her wrath. Such a calm, kind, earnest expression in the mild blue eyes, such a winning smile played round the handsome mouth, a more prepossessing countenance Isabel had never seen, there was something about it irresistibly attractive. "What is it you wish me to do," she asked as her eyes met his.

"Stay where you are, and do just the same as if I was not here he said, and not run off as if I was going to eat you."

"Then don't talk about me," she returned stiffly.

"I'm sure. I never said a word about you."

"But the children did," she replied coloring deeply as she returned to her seat.

"Please Everard wont you read to us?" asked Amy.

When he had finished, Amy asked Isabel if she would play the hymn she promised.

"Not to-night dear," replied Isabel.

"Oh please, Miss Leicester," coaxed Rose.

"If I am the cause of their disappointment I will go, but indeed I should like to join," said Everard.

"As you please" said Isabel, ashamed of being so much out of temper.

"You know you promised, Miss Leicester," interposed Alice, gravely.

"So I did, dear," returned Isabel, going to the piano: and she was quite repaid, as they all sang very sweetly, and quite correctly.

"Good night," said Everard, when the hymn was ended.

"Forgive me, Miss Leicester if I seemed rude, I did not intend to be."

Isabel was distressed to find how much the children had been neglected; true they were tolerably proficient in their studies, but in all religious instruction they were miserably deficient.

Left entirely to the care of Miss Manning, who was a very frivolous, worldly minded woman, they were led, (tho' perhaps unintentionally) to regard all religious subjects as dry and tedious, and to be avoided as much as possible. Isabel determined to try and remedy this evil by the exercise of patient gentleness, and by striving to make religious instruction a pleasure and a privilege. No easy task did this appear considering the dispositions she had to deal with, nor was it without a struggle that she put aside her own wishes and devoted her Sunday afternoons to this purpose. She certainly did not meet with much encouragement at first; again and again did the question recur to her mind, what good am I doing, why should I deprive myself of so many pleasant hours for the benefit of these thankless children; but the selfish thought was conquered, and she persevered. On week days also, she had morning prayer and read a portion of scripture, then they sung a hymn, always taking for the week the one they learnt on the Sunday afternoon. Nor was her perseverance unavailing, for the children became interested, and requested her to have evening service as they termed it, which of course Isabel was only too glad to do. After a while their morning numbers were increased, as Emily and her papa joined them, and so on until at last without any special arrangement they all assembled in the school-room every morning as a matter of course.

Isabel was very different from what Mrs. Arlington had expected, so refined in her manners and tastes, so totally unfitted to combat with all the mortifications of a governess's career. True, she had expected a rather superior person, when Mrs. Arnold wrote that Miss Leicester was the indulged daughter of a wealthy merchant, who on account of her father's losses and subsequent death, was forced to gain her living by teaching. Still, she was not prepared to find her new governess such a lovely and sweet tempered girl, and Isabel had not been long at Elm Grove, before Mrs. Arlington found that she was becoming quite attached to her. And as Mr. Arlington found that her father was the same Mr. Leicester from whom he had formerly experienced great kindness, they decided Isabel should teach the children, and receive her salary, but that in all other respects she should be as one of the family, and Isabel was very glad of the change.

CHAPTER IV

The winter was past, and it was now June—bright, sunny June—and Elm Grove was decked in its richest hues. Down from the house sloped a beautiful lawn, studded with shrubs, and adorned with flower-beds of different sizes and shapes; while in the centre there was a pond and fountain, with a weeping willow shading the sunny side, which gave an appearance of coolness quite refreshing. Beyond was the shrubbery and fruit garden; and to the left the meadow, bounded by a coppice.

The house was of the gothic order: on the right side of it was a beautiful conservatory, filled with the choicest plants; on the left a colonnade and terrace, shaded by a group of acacia trees. In front a piazza and large portico, around which honeysuckle, clematis and roses, shed their sweet perfume. The grounds were tastefully laid out, with due regard to shade; and a grove of elm trees completely hid the house from the avenue: so that in approaching it from the main road, the house seemed still in the distance—even out of sight—until, on taking a half turn round a thick clump of elms, one would unexpectedly come out right in front of the house, almost at the door. It was, as Emily had said, a delightful place.

The children had greatly improved under Isabel's care. Emily

Clotilda Jennings

was quite like a sister, and even Miss Arlington treated her as an equal. Isabel knew that governesses were not usually so fortunate as to meet with such nice people, and appreciated their kindness accordingly. The walks, too, that she had so much dreaded, had become a pleasure,—not a disagreeable duty. Emily usually joined them, and not unfrequently Everard also. He performed almost impossibilities to get Isabel wild-flowers, of which, Rose had informed him, she was exceedingly fond. These, to his great annoyance, were always carefully deposited in a glass on the dining-room table; for Isabel had remarked in his manner toward her more than mere politeness, and endeavored as much as possible to check his growing attentions. But all his acts of kindness were done with so much tact and consideration, as to leave her no alternative, and oblige her to receive them. Neither was there anything in his behaviour or conversation that she could complain of, or that others would remark. All this made it very difficult for her to know how to act, as she did not wish to hurt his feelings by unnecessary particularity, or by the assumption of unusual formality lead him to suspect the true cause; and thus perhaps lay herself open to the possibility of being supposed to have imagined him to be in love with her, without due cause. Isabel knew that she was not deceived; she knew also that she must be very careful to conceal that she was so well aware of the state of his feelings towards her.

"The Morningtons are coming to stay at Ashton Park: are you not glad, Emmy?" said Everard, as he joined Isabel, Emily, and the children, in their ramble, one bright day in the midsummer holidays. "Glad, I should think so!" returned Emily; "but when do they come?"

"Very soon, I believe; and I expect we shall have jolly times. Harry's so full of life, and that merry little Lucy is the spirit of fun. May will be here shortly. And the Harringtons have friends with them, so we shall be able to get up some nice picnics."

"But is not Ada coming?" asked Emily.

"Why, of course she is," returned Everard; "but if you have not heard the 'latest,' I shall not enlighten you sister mine."

"O Everard! I'm all curiosity," cried Emily, opening her blue eyes very wide.

"You mean that Ada is engaged to Mr. Ashton," said Isabel.

"Yes; but how on earth did you know it?" he returned.

"Do you know the Morningtons?" asked Emily. "Have you known them long?"

"Longer than you have, I fancy," replied Isabel. "I have known them as long as I can remember. Ada and I had the same room at school. She is my dearest and most intimate friend."

"I suppose you know Harry and the rest very well?"

"O yes, we were quite like brothers and sisters,"

"When are they expected?" asked Emily.

"They may be there already, for all I know. It was last Sunday Sir John told papa they were coming."

At this moment Charles Ashton, with Ada and Lucy Mornington, emerged from a bridle path through the woods that separated Elm Grove from Ashton Park. Greetings were warmly exchanged, and then amid a cross-fire of questions and small talk, they proceeded to the house, where they found Mrs. Mornington and Lady Ashton. The latter insisted upon the young ladies and Everard returning with them to spend a few days at the Park.

Isabel declined to accompany them. At which, Lucy fairly shed tears, and every one seemed so much annoyed, that she finally consented.

Her position of friend and governess combined, when alone, was pleasant enough; but with strangers, of course, she was still only Mrs. Arlington's governess, and was treated accordingly. That is, when it was known; as people at first did not usually suppose that the beautiful and attractive Miss Leicester was only the governess. And Isabel was sometimes amused, as well as annoyed, to find people who had been very friendly, cool off perceptibly. This she attributed to the circumstance that she was 'only the governess.' Lady Ashton, especially, had been very anxious to be introduced to that "charming Miss Leicester;" and Isabel had afterwards heard her saying to a friend: "Well! you surprise me! So she is 'only the governess,' and yet has the air of a princess. I'm sure I thought she was 'somebody.' But then, you know, there are persons who don't seem to know their proper place." All this had made Isabel cold and reserved in company; for her high spirit could ill brook the slights and patronising airs of those who in other days would have been glad of her acquaintance.

Thus Isabel was deemed haughty and cold; few, if any, perceiving that this cold reserve was assumed to hide how deeply these things wounded her too sensitive feelings. So it was with more pain than pleasure that she made one of the party to Ashton Park, having a presentiment that vexation and annoyance would be the result; as she was quite sure that it was only to please Ada, that Lady Ashton had included her in the invitation.

Nor did it tend to disperse these gloomy apprehensions, when Isabel found that the room assigned her was at the extreme end of the corridor, scantily, even meanly furnished, and had apparently been long unoccupied, as, although it was now June, there was something damp, chilly, and uncomfortable about it. During the whole of this visit, she was destined to suffer from annoyances of one kind or another. If there was a spooney, or country cousin, among the guests, Lady Ashton would be sure to bring him to Miss Leicester, and whisper her to amuse him if possible, and she would greatly oblige. So that Isabel scarcely ever enjoyed herself. Or just as some expedition was being arranged, Lady Ashton would, by employing Isabel about her flowers, or some other trivial thing, contrive to keep her from making one of the party. Isabel, though intensely disgusted, was too proud to remonstrate. And even when Charles, once or twice, interfered to prevent her being kept at home, she felt almost inclined to refuse, so annoyed and angry did Lady Ashton appear.

True, she might have had some enjoyment from the society of Harry and Everard. But so surely as Lady Ashton observed either of them in conversation with her, she invariably wanted to introduce them to some 'charming young ladies.' And she took good care that Isabel should not join any of the riding parties. Once Arthur Barrington had particularly requested her to do so, and even offered his own horse (as Lady Ashton had assured them that every horse that could carry a lady had already been appropriated), but his aunt interposed: "O my dear Arthur, if you would only be so good as to lend it to poor little Mary Cleavers! Of course I would not have ventured to suggest your giving up your horse; but as you are willing to do so, I must put in a claim for poor little Mary, who is almost breaking her heart at the idea of staying at home. And Miss Leicester is so good-natured, that I am sure she will not object."

"Excuse me, aunt, but"—began Arthur.

"Here! Mary, dear," cried Lady Ashton; and before Arthur could finish the sentence, his aunt had informed Mary that he had kindly promised his horse. Mary turned, and overwhelmed the astonished Arthur with her profuse thanks.

"Confound it," muttered Arthur (who was too much a gentleman to contradict his aunt and make a scene); then bowing politely to Miss Cleaver, he turned to Isabel, saying, "Will you come for a row on the lake, Miss Leicester, as our riding to-day is now out of the question, as my aunt has monopolized 'Archer' so unceremoniously. I feel assured that Miss Lucy will join us, as she is not one of the riding party."

Isabel assented, and Arthur went in search of Lucy.

Lady Ashton followed him, and remonstrated: "You know you were to be one of the riding party, Arthur."

"Impossible, my dear aunt. After what has passed, I can't do less than devote my time this morning to the service of Miss Leicester."

"Nonsense; she is 'only a governess.'"

"So much the more would she feel any slight."

"You talk absurdly," she returned with a sneer. "You can't take her alone, Arthur. I will not allow it."

"My dear aunt, I am much too prudent for that. Lucy Mornington goes with us."

"But who will ride with Mary?"

"Oh, you must get her a cavalier, as you did a horse, I suppose," he returned carelessly. At all events, I am not at her service, even though no other be found;" and he passed on toward Lucy, regardless of his aunt's displeasure. And he carried the day in spite of her, for she put in practice several little schemes to prevent Isabel going. But Lady Ashton was defeated; and Isabel remembered this morning as the only really pleasant time during her stay at the Park.

Lady Ashton was greatly perplexed as to how to procure a beau for Mary, and, as a last resource, pressed Sir John into service; but as he was a very quiet, stately old gentleman, the ride, to poor Mary's great chagrin, was a very formal affair.

On the last evening of her stay at Ashton Park, Isabel was admiring the beautiful sunset from her window, and as she stood lost in reverie, someone entered hastily and fastened the door. Turning to see who the intruder might be, she beheld a very beautiful girl, apparently about fourteen years of age, her large eyes flashing with anger, while her short, quick breathing, told of excitement and disquietude. "I have had such a dance to get here without observation," she panted forth. "Please let me stay a little while." And before Isabel could recover from her momentary surprise, Louisa had thrown herself into her arms, exclaiming, "I knew that you were kind and good, or I would not have come, and I felt sure that you would pity me." All anger was now gone from the eager, earnest face, raised imploringly, and Isabel's sympathy was aroused by the weary, sad expression of her countenance.

"Who are you; what makes you unhappy; and why do you seek my sympathy?" asked Isabel.

"I am Lady Ashton's grand-daughter, Louisa Aubray," she replied. "You don't know what a life I lead, boxed up with old Grumps, and strictly forbidden all other parts of the house. I have been here two years, and during all that time I have not had any pleasure or liberty, except once or twice when I took French leave, when I was sure of not being found out. Ah, you don't know how miserable I am! no one cares for poor Louisa;" and burying her face in her hands, she cried bitterly. "I sometimes watch the company going to dinner, and that was how I came to see you; and I liked you the best of them all, and I wished so much to speak to you. So I managed to find out which was your room; but it was only to-day that I could get here, unknown to Miss Crosse. Won't you please tell me which of those young ladies Uncle Charles is going to marry. I want so much to know; because Uncle Charles is nice, and I like him. He is the only one here that ever was the least bit kind to me. As for grandpapa and grandmamma, I know they hate me; and Eliza says, that the reason grandpapa can't bear the sight of me, is because I am like papa. Oh, I know that dear mamma would not have been so glad when they promised to take care of me, if she had known how unkind they would be."

"But how can I help you, dear?" inquired Isabel.

"Why, I thought if I told you, you would be sorry for me, and persuade grandmamma to send me to school; for then, at least, I should have someone to speak to. I don't mind study,—only old Miss Crosse is so unkind. I think perhaps she might, if you were to coax her very much—do please," said Louisa, warmly.

Isabel smiled at the idea that she should be thought to have any influence with Lady Ashton. "You err greatly, dear child, in thinking that I have any power to help you. I can only advise you to try and bear your present trials, and wait patiently for better times," she said.

"Ah, it's all very well for you to tell me this. You have all you can wish, and everything nice, so it is easy to give advice; but you wouldn't like it, I can tell you."

"I don't expect you to like it, Louisa. I only want you to make the best of what can't be helped."

"Oh, but it might be helped, if you would only try," urged Louisa.

"It is getting late," returned Isabel, "and I must now dress for dinner; but if you like you may remain here while I do so, and I will tell you about a young lady that I know, and then perhaps you will not be so annoyed with me for giving you the advice I have."

"Thanks," returned Louisa, "I should like it very much."

"This young lady's parents were very rich, and indulged her in every way. Her mother died when she was only eight years old. Her father had her taught every accomplishment, and instructed in almost every branch of learning. And she lived in a beautiful house, surrounded by every luxury, until the age of nineteen, when her father died; and as he lost all his property shortly before, she was forced to gain her living as a governess. Think what she must have suffered, who never in her life had had a harsh or unkind word, and scarcely ever had a wish ungratified; but had been spoilt and petted at home, and courted and flattered abroad. Think what it must have been to go alone and friendless among strangers; to earn, by the irksome task of teaching, no more a year than she had been accustomed to receive in a birthday present or Xmas gift. She was fortunate enough to meet with very kind people, who made her as comfortable as it was possible for her to be under the circumstances. But still she found her position a very trying one, and was often placed in very unpleasant circumstances, and sometimes met with great mortifications. And that young lady, Louisa,—is myself."

"Oh! I'm sorry, so sorry," exclaimed Louisa. "And I thought you so happy, and so much to be envied. And I'm sorry also for what I said about it being so easy to give advice. But why don't you marry some rich gentleman? and then, you know, you needn't be a governess any more. I would."

"I didn't say that I was unhappy, Louisa, and I try not to let these things trouble me so much, for I know it is wrong to care so much about them, but I can't help it. I have not told you this to excite your pity; but that you may know that others have their daily trials as well as yourself. Do not think, dear child, that I do not compassionate your sad lot; only try to remember the comforts which you do enjoy, notwithstanding the ills you are called upon to endure. Think how much worse your fate might have been, if your grand-parents had refused to provide for you; and be sure if you have patience, and do what is right, in due time you will have your reward."

Louisa was now weeping violently. "Ah, you don't, you can't know, what it is to live as I do. And I felt so sure that— you—could help me; but you can't, I know now, for grandmamma wouldn't listen to 'a governess.' She is so bitter against anyone that teaches, because of papa. But I can't, and won't, stand this miserable life much longer—I will not!" she continued passionately, as with compressed lips and clenched hands she started to her feet, while the angry flashing eyes and determined countenance told of strong will and firm resolution. "If I was a boy," she said, "I would run away and go to sea; but I am only a girl, and there is so little that a girl can do. But I will find some way to escape before long, if things continue like this—that I will!" and she stamped her foot impatiently upon the ground. Isabel could scarcely believe that the passionate girl before her was indeed the same child who had sat at her side so meekly not a moment before. She no longer paid any attention to Louisa's complaints. Her thoughts were far away with the only one in whom she had ever seen this sudden transition from persuasive gentleness to stormy anger; for the proud, passionate girl brought him vividly to her mind, though the wide ocean rolled between them. She saw again the proud curling lip, and the dark expressive eyes, which one moment would beam on her in love, and the next flash with angry light and stern displeasure; the haughty mien and proud defiance, blended with a strange fascinating gentleness, that had won her heart. The time was present to her imagination, when with passionate entreaty he had urged upon her the necessity for a secret marriage, and in fondest accents implored her not to refuse, as he was positive that her father would never consent to their union; and his fearful burst of passion when she most entirely, though tearfully, refused to accede to his request. Even now she trembled as she recalled the angry terms in which he reproached her, and the indignant manner in which he had expressed his conviction that she did not love him; and that all henceforth was at an end between them. How he left her in great wrath; but soon after returned, and in the most humble manner deplored his cruelty and hateful temper, and in gentlest strains implored her forgiveness. But her musings were rather abruptly terminated by Louisa exclaiming: "Oh! tell me what is the matter. Your hand is quite cold, and you are trembling all over. What have I done? what shall I do?" she continued, wringing her hands in despair.

"I cannot talk to you any more now, Louisa dear," replied Isabel, "but I will tell Ada about you, and perhaps she may be able to help you; but you really must not get into such dreadful passions. I can't have you stay any longer, as I wish to be alone."

"But why do you tremble and look so pale?" asked Louisa, mournfully. "Is it so dreadful to be a governess?"

"I was not thinking of that dear," answered Isabel, kissing her "good-night. Mind you try to be a good girl."

So Louisa was dismissed, fully persuaded in her own mind that she had nearly frightened Isabel to death by her passionate behaviour.

After waiting a moderate time to recover herself, Isabel joined the others in the drawing-room. Fortunately, they went to dinner almost immediately, as she felt anything but inclined to make herself agreeable; and as Lady Ashton, as usual, was kind enough to furnish her with a companion who appeared to be a quiet, inoffensive individual, she treated him with polite indifference. She was deceived, however, in her opinion regarding Mr. Lascelles. The man was an 'ass,' and a 'magpie,' and appeared to like nothing better than to hear his own voice. However, this suited Isabel tolerably on this occasion, as an 'indeed,' or 'really,' was all that was needed by way of reply; and he was forced sometimes to stop to enable him to eat, and this kept him from being oppressive. But as he found her so good a listener, there was no getting rid of him; for when the gentlemen joined the ladies in the drawing-room, he devoted himself entirely to Miss Leicester—to Lucy's intense amusement. At last Ada grew compassionate, and got Charles to ask Isabel to sing, and to introduce Mr. Lascelles to Miss Cleaver. It was a tedious evening, and Isabel was heartily glad that they were to return to Elm Grove. Life there was at all events endurable, which the life she had spent for the last week was certainly not. She was sick and tired of hearing the oft-repeated question and answer, "Who is that young lady?"— "Oh, the governess at Elm Grove;" and most emphatically determined that she would never stay at the Park again, let who might be offended.

Neither could she help drawing comparisons between this and her former life, nor deny that she felt it severely. But the warm welcome she received from the children on her return to the Grove, went far towards dispersing these gloomy thoughts.

CHAPTER V

A pic-nic was decided upon for Emily's birthday—the fourth of August. It was a lovely day, and every thing seemed propitious. And a merrier party seldom started on a pleasure excursion, than the one which now was assembled under the trees at Elm Grove. The guests were Sir John and Lady Ashton, Charles, and the Morningtons, Lilly and Peter Rosecrain, May Arlington (a cousin), the Harringtons and the Hon. Arthur Barrington, the latter had not arrived, but had promised to meet them at their destination. Emily was in ecstasy, and the children quite wild with delight. All Isabel's endeavors to keep them in order were useless, and Lucy announced, that every one must be allowed to do just as he or she pleased, or there would be no fun. Lucy volunteered to go with the children if they could procure a driver. "Any one would do, excepting Mr. Everard Arlington, as of course the children would be too much in awe of him, as he could be awefully grave."

Peter immediately offered his services, unless he was too stern and sedate. This caused a laugh, as Peter was renowned for fun.

The place chosen for the pic-nic was a delightful spot, (quite romantic Emily declared) situated at the bottom of a beautiful ravine, within a short distance of a splendid water fall yclept the "old roar," the dashing spray of its gurgling waters making quite refreshing music.

"Now Emily, you are queen to-day, and all that you say is law," cried the laughing Lucy, when they arrived at their destination. "Now master Bob, be on your P's and Q's, and find a nice place to spread the royal feast."

"I think that you are making yourself queen on this occasion and no mistake," returned the saucy Bob.

"Well, I am prime minister you know, so make haste and obey my commands."

"Self constituted I fancy," returned Bob with a shrug.

"May I ask what important office is to be assigned me on this festive occasion," asked Peter.

"That of queen's jester, of course," replied Lucy gravely.

"You do me too much honor Miss Lucy," he said, bowing with mock humility.

"I'm quite aware of that," answered Lucy demurely.

A desirable place was soon found in a shady nook, and the repast was spread, to which it is almost needless to add they all did ample justice.

Just as they sat down, Arthur made his appearance, bringing Louisa Aubray with him. If a look could have done it Lady Ashton would have annihilated him, so fearfully angry was she at his daring to bring her grand daughter in this manner, upon his own responsibility.

"I found Louisa very disconsolate and unhappy, and I thought a little recreation would be good for her, Aunty. I feel sure that Mrs. Arlington will excuse the liberty I have taken," he added with a smile and bow.

"Pray don't mention it, replied Mrs. Arlington thus appealed to, I am only too happy to have Miss Aubray join us. Alice my dear, make room for Miss Aubray."

Louisa sat with her large mournful eyes cast down, tho' occasionally she threw furtive glances at her grandmother's darkened countenance, and seemed to be doing anything but enjoying herself. And no wonder poor child, for she was sure of a terrible scolding sooner or later. Arthur paid attention to the ladies generally, with whom he was a great favorite.

Louisa ate her dinner almost in silence, tho' Alice did her best to draw her out. But poor girl, she was calculating the chances of being left alone with her angry grandmother when they dispersed after dinner, and almost wished she had not yielded to Arthur's persuasions, as he had apparently deserted her. But he was much too considerate and kind hearted for that, he had brought her there to enjoy herself, and it would not be his fault if she didn't. They began dispersing by twos and threes to explore the beauties of the place, and Louisa's heart sank within her, as she saw their numbers diminishing fast, and that Arthur too had disappeared.

The children asked Isabel to come and see Rose's bower, and after a short consultation, Alice invited Louisa to join them, but Lady Ashton interposed.

"I had much rather you remained with me my dear," she said curtly. And Louisa reseated herself with a great sigh as the others started on their ramble. For the children had much too great an awe of Lady Ashton, to attempt to intercede on Louisa's behalf, and if the truth must be told, they didn't much care for her company. So Louisa was left alone with the elders, who were not in such haste to move after their repast as the young people.

"Come Louisa, let us follow the example of the rest," said Arthur reappearing.

"I have ordered Louisa to remain here, interposed Lady Ashton sternly."

"Oh! Aunt," remonstrated Arthur.

"I don't approve of her coming at all, but as she is here she—"

"May as well enjoy herself," put in Arthur.

"Arthur," ejaculated Lady Ashton, in her most freezing tone.

"But Aunt," you see that she is the only young lady left, and you wouldn't be so cruel as to condemn me to wander alone through these picturesque ravines."

"You can stay here, and amuse us old people," returned Lady Ashton grimly.

Arthur shrugged his shoulders and elevated his eye-brows, by way of reply.

"Oh! that is too much to expect," interposed Mrs. Arlington kindly, "I think you should relent Josephine."

"But you know that I refused to let her go with Miss Leicester and the children."

"Oh! did you," interrupted Arthur, "that was too bad."

"Come Louisa, we will try and find them," and off he marched her from under Lady Ashton's very nose, as Louisa felt bold with Arthur to back her, and she knew that she could not increase the weight of censure already incured— she also longed to get out of her grandmother's presence on any terms.

Rose's bower (so called from Rose having been the first to discover it) was some distance up the winding path. It was a nice little nook, thickly shaded on all sides, having a small aperture in the west, and was completely covered with wild flowers of every description. The ascent was very difficult, for they had quite to force their way through the underwood. They arrived at last, tired and breathless, but the wild secluded beauty of the spot quite repaid them for their trouble. Isabel was in raptures, and expressed her admiration in no measured terms to the delighted children.

"Oh! Everard, how did you find us," exclaimed Alice, as that gentleman made his appearance, "I thought no one knew of this place but ourselves."

"Oh I followed just to see to what unheard of spot you were taking Miss Leicester," replied Everard good-naturedly.

"Then you might have joined us, and not have crept after us in that mean way." said Rose angrily.

"Rose, my dear Rose, you must not speak in that way." interposed Isabel authoritatively.

"Oh Rose, don't you like Everard to come," asked Amy reproachfully.

"I don't like him to come in that way." returned Rose.

"Wouldn't you like to gather some of those black berries," asked Everard, after they had rested a while.

"O yes," they all exclaimed, "what beauties," and off they scampered. Isabel was about to follow, but Everard interposed, "Stay, Miss Leicester, I have long sought an opportunity to address you, and can no longer delay—I must speak—"

Isabel would have made her escape, but that Everard stood between her and the only available opening. She knew that he was about to propose, and would gladly have prevented it if possible, but as it was, there was no reprieve—he would do it.

How signally had she failed, notwithstanding all her efforts, for she could not but feel, that she had not succeeded in making clear to him, her own ideas on the subject, or this would not have been. How sorry she was now, that she had allowed the fear of being unnecessarily cool to influence her conduct,—yet at the same time, she could not accuse herself of having given him any encouragement. Yet, how far was he from anticipating a refusal, and how unprepared to receive it. She saw it, there was no doubt manifested in the eager expressive eyes, in the warm impulsive manner blended with a gentle earnestness that might have won the heart of a girl whose affections were disengaged. He looked so handsome, so loveable, that Isabel felt she might indeed have been content to take him, had not her affections been given to another, and she grieved to think of the pain she must inflict.

It might have been easier if he had not looked so bright and hopeful about it, or if she could have told him of her

Clotilda Jennings

engagement, but that was out of the question, he seemed so certain of success, so utterly unconscious of the fate that awaited him, that she could have wept, but resolutely repressing her tears, she waited with heightening color to hear the words that were to be so kindly, yet so vainly spoken.

"Dearest Isabel," he said in accents soft and winning. "I have loved you ever since I first saw you on that Sunday afternoon, and all that I have seen of you since, has only increased my esteem. But of late you have been more retiring than formerly, and I have even thought that you avoided me sometimes, thinking I fear, that my attentions (to use a common phrase) meant nothing, but that is not the case, I am not one of those, who merely to gratify their own vanity, would endeavor to win affection, which they do not,— cannot return. No dearest, I love you truly, unalterably,— will you then accept my love, and give me the right and the inexpressibly pleasure to share all your joys and sorrows. Tell me dear Isabel, will you be my wife."

She was trembling—almost gasping, and he would have aided her with his supporting arm, but she sank away from him sobbing "It can never, never be."

"Why do you say that Isabel," he asked reproachfully, while the expression of his countenance became that of unmitigated sorrow.

"Even could I return your affection," she answered more calmly, "It would not be right to accept you under the circumstances. Your parents would consider, that as their governess, I ought to know my duty better."

"What difference could your being the governess make," he asked.

"Every difference in their opinion."

"But as I am the only son, of course they would raise no objection."

"That makes it the more certain that they would do so," she replied.

"Oh! Isabel" he exclaimed passionately, "do not reason in this cool way, when my whole life will be happy or miserable as you make it. I am not changeable, I shall not cease to love you while I live."

"Oh! do not say that I have so much influence upon your happiness Mr. Arlington," returned Isabel much affected. "You must not think of me otherwise than as a friend, a kind friend—a dear friend if you will, but I can never be anything more."

"Oh! Isabel, dear Isabel, do not refuse me thus, you do not know, indeed you do not, how true a heart you are crushing, what fervent love you are rejecting. Only let me hope that time may change your feelings."

"Do not think that I undervalue the love you offer, but it is impossible—quite impossible that we can ever be more to each other than at present. I would not raise false hopes or allow you to indulge them. I do not, cannot return your affections, I can never be your wife, it is utterly impossible."

"You love another Isabel, else why impossible. Perhaps, even now you are the promised bride of another, tell me if this is the case," he said tho' his voice faltered.

"You are presuming Mr. Arlington, you have no right to ask this question," she replied with glowing cheeks.

"Pardon me if I have offended," he said.

"I think that this interview has lasted long enough—too long in fact. I will now join the children if you please."

"One moment more, say that we do not part in anger."

"In anger, no, we are good friends I trust," she answered, smiling very sweetly.

"My dream of happiness is over," he said sadly, almost tearfully as he took her offered hand.

Isabel had some difficulty in finding the children on such a wild place. When she did so, she found Arthur and Louisa with them. Louisa was looking bright and animated, very different to what she had done during dinner, and was laughing and joining in the general conversation.

"We are taking Mr. Barrington and Louisa to the bower," cried Rose as they drew near.

"I'm afraid we shall be rather late," answered Isabel.

"But you surely wouldn't have us return without seeing this wonderful bower, after undergoing all this fatigue," inquired Arthur.

"Certainly not, but I would rather be excused climbing up there again to-day. I will wait here until you come back." returned Isabel.

"Where is Everard." asked Alice.

"I left him at the bower,"

"I think I will wait with Miss Leicester," said Amy, "I'm so very tired."

"Yes do," cried Rose, "for then we shall not be half so long gone."

Isabel sat down on the lovely green sward, and the tired child reclined beside her. Amy was so thoroughly worn out that she lay perfectly quiet, and Isabel was left to her own reflections, and these were by no means pleasant. Her conversation with Everard had cast a gloom over her spirits, she no longer took pleasure in the ramble or in the beautiful scenery around her, all the brightness of the day was gone, and why, he was not the first rejected suitor, but she had never felt like this with regard to the others. But then she had been the rich Miss Leicester, and it was so easy to imagine that she was courted for her wealth, but in the present instance it was different. Nothing but true disinterested love could have prompted him, and she felt hurt and grieved to think that she was the object of such warm affection to one who she esteemed so highly, when her affections were already engaged. She had seen how deeply her answer pained him, yet had not dared to answer his question. Could she tell him what she had not dared to reveal to her dying father? No; tho' could she have done so, it might have made it easier for Everard to forget her. When they reached the place of rendezvous, they found the rest of the party including Everard, already assembled, and Peter was declaring that it was utterly impossible to return without having some refreshments, after the immense fatigue they had all undergone in exploring the beauties of the surrounding country. Most of the party were of the same opinion, so forthwith he and Bob Mornington proceeded to ransack the hampers, and distributed the contents in the most primitive manner imaginable, to the amusement of the company generally, and to the extreme disgust of Grace Arlington in

Clotilda Jennings

particular. And then there was a general move to the carriages. After they arrived at Elm Grove, Lady Ashton insisted upon Louisa returning to the park at once. Several voices were raised in her behalf, but in vain, Lady Ashton was inexorable, and telling Louisa to say good bye to Mrs. Arlington, she hurried her away, and desired Sunmers the coachman to drive Miss Aubray home and return for her at twelve.

Arthur followed and remonstrated.

"Arthur, say no more," returned Lady Ashton decisively. "I consider you took a great liberty in bringing her, and I will not allow her to remain."

"Since you are quite sure that it is best for her to go, I will drive her home, she need not go alone in the great carriage, like a naughty child sent home in disgrace," he answered laughing.

"Nonsense, Arthur, don't be so absurd," said Lady Ashton tartly.

"Indeed my dear Aunt, as I persuaded her to come I positively could not have her treated so unceremoniously," he replied. "Here Thomson," he called to the man who was about to take Archer to the stable, and the next moment he had handed the mistified Louisa into the chaise, leaving the astonished Lady Ashton crimson with rage.

"Adieu Aunty" he cried, gathering up the ribbons, "I must trust to you to make my apologies to Mrs. Arlington, and off he drove. Lady Ashton re-entered the house, inwardly vowing vengeance against the unlucky Louisa, tho' she met Mrs. Arlington with a smile, saying, "that Arthur had begged her to apologize, as he had thought it incumbent upon him to drive his cousin home, as it was entirely his fault that she had come, and you know," she added with a little laugh, "how scrupulously polite he is to every one—."

To Lady Ashton's great chagrin, this was the last that was seen of Arthur at Elm Grove that night, and she would have been still more annoyed had she known how thoroughly he and Louisa were enjoying themselves over their game of chess, notwithstanding Miss Crosse's exemplary vigilance.

The evening was spent in various amusements, and the company dispersed at a late hour, all highly satisfied, and voting the pic-nic a complete success.

After the guests had departed, Isabel had occasion to go into the school-room for a book, and as the beautiful harvest moon was shining so brightly, she stood a moment at the open window to enjoy the lovely prospect. Hearing some one enter the room, she turned and encountered Everard. She would have retreated, but Everard gently detained her, "promise me Miss Leicester," he said, "that what passed between us this afternoon shall make no difference to your arrangements, you will not think of leaving, for I should never forgive myself for having deprived my sisters of the benefit of your society if you do."

"I could scarcely do so if I wished," she replied with a sigh.

"Only say that you do not wish it," returned Everard earnestly.

"I do not, you have all been so kind, so very kind to me, that I should be very sorry to leave, nor could I do so very easily as I have no home."

"Dear Isabel, why not accept the home I offer you?"

Clotilda Jennings

"Stay Mr. Arlington, say no more. You must promise not to recur to that subject again, or however unpleasant it may be to do so, I shall have no alternative, but must seek another situation."

"I will make it a forbidden subject while you remain at Elm Grove if you wish it," he said doubtfully.

"It must be so Mr. Arlington; good night."

When Isabel entered her own room she found Emily there.

"Dear Isabel," she said, after seating herself on a low stool at Isabel's feet, "what a delightful day this has been, O I'm so happy," and she hid her face in Isabel's lap. "I cannot go to Grace, so I come to you," she continued, "You are more sympathetic and seem to understand me better. Not but what Grace has always been kind enough, but I always am rather in awe of her, and you have just been the friend I always wanted. Oh! Isabel, you don't know how much good you have done me. You have taught me to think more of right and wrong, and to consider duty as well as pleasure, and to think of others as well as myself. I know now, that Miss Massie was right when she said that I was wilful and selfish, and had no consideration for others, tho' at the time she said it I thought her severe and unjust. Before you came here, I made up my mind to be kind to you, and to try to like you, (tho' I own that I thought it very improbable that I should do so in reality) but you know, my Godmother Mrs. Arnold had written me, that I must be kind to you and love you, under pain of her displeasure, but when I saw how pretty you were, I thought it would not be a difficult task. Now I have learned to love you for yourself, because you are good as well as beautiful."

"Oh! stop, you little flatterer, you will make me vain," said

Isabel kissing her. "If I have done you any good, I am very glad indeed," she added in a more serious tone, "I have endeavored to do my duty, but I am afraid that I have not succeeded very well."

"O yes, indeed you have, but what do you think that I came here to tell you dear."

Isabel confessed that it was useless to attempt to guess as the day had been such an eventful one, and offered so large a scope for the imagination.

"Well if you won't guess I must tell you deary, I'm engaged to Harry Mornington."

"May you be very, very happy dear Emily," said Isabel returning her embrace. Then, unable any longer to sustain the composure she had forced herself to assume, she laid her head upon Emily's shoulder and wept passionately.

"What can make this affect you thus," asked the amazed and astonished Emily, greatly distressed, "Oh! Isabel is it possible that you love him, how unfortunate that I should have chosen you for my confidant, but I didn't know, I never thought, or believe me I would not have pained you thus. You said that he had always been like a brother to you, how could I know that you ever thought he would be anything more. Indeed, she added as if to vindicate Harry, "I never saw anything in his manner to lead you to suppose so."

"You are quite mistaken dear Emily," interposed Isabel, as soon as she could control her sobs sufficiently to give utterance to the words "I never thought or wished that Harry should ever be more to me than the dear friend he has ever been. But I have many sources of trouble that you are not aware of dear Emily, and to-day, while others laughed, I could have wept, and would gladly have exchanged that gay scene, for the quiet of my own room. But this could not be, and I was forced to assume a serenity of feeling I was far from experiencing. Had you not been here, I should have given vent to my grief in solitude, and none would have been the wiser. As it is I must entreat that you will forgive me for (tho' unintentionally) making you suppose I do not sympathize in your happiness, but I do indeed, for I know that Harry is all that is good, and is worthy of your best affections."

"Dear Isabel, will you not tell me your troubles," inquired Emily, "for ills lose half their weight by being shared with another."

"I cannot tell you dear, but for the present I will forget my uneasiness in sharing your happiness."

Then after a long and pleasant conversation they parted, both amazed at the late, or rather early hour which at that moment struck.

"By-the-bye," said Emily, coming back after a few minutes "papa gave me this letter for you two days ago, but I quite forgot it until I saw it just now."

"O you naughty, naughty girl," cried Isabel, looking very bright as she beheld the familiar epistle.

"No more tears to-night I fancy, eh Isabel," said Emily saucily. "Don't sit up to read it to-night, it is so very late," she added wickedly, her eyes sparkling with mischief.

All else was soon forgotten as Isabel eagerly perused the welcome letter from her own Louis, whose silence had been one source of her disquietude. But Louis accounted for his silence to her entire satisfaction, and promised to send an extra one at an early date.

Clotilda Jennings

CHAPTER VI

Isabel was to spend this Xmas with the Morningtons, who with with the exception of Harry, were to return to Europe in February. It was very rough weather, and Isabel had much such a journey as that to Elm Grove, and was in a very similar condition to what she had been on that occasion. On her arrival at Eastwood, Ada embracing her exclaimed "Oh! here you are at last my own darling Isabel, I have been watching for you all day, papa was sadly afraid of accidents this stormy weather, and Bob kept bringing such dreadful accounts of trains being snowed up, that he nearly frightened me to death. Papa has been to the depot three times, and Harry twice, and missed you after all. But do come and warm yourself dearest, for you seem half frozen," she continued as she hurried Isabel into the cosy little breakfast-room, where the bright fire was indeed a pleasant sight on such a bitterly cold day.

"We met with several disagreeable stoppages, but nothing worse" replied Isabel, her teeth chattering with cold. "I am sadly chilled with this piercing wind, Oh! this is nice" she added going to the fire, "and it is so very pleasant to be at 'Eastwood' once more."

"Why here is Isabel I declare," cried the impulsive Lucy, as she bounded into the room, "how delightful, you will help me to arrange the gim-cracks on the Xmas tree, won't you my pet," said the merry girl as she threw her arms round her friend, and hugged her unmercifully.

"To be sure I will, when I recover the use of my fingers," returned Isabel laughing.

"Well, I don't want you to come now, for if I am a little madcap as papa says, I'm not quite so unreasonable as that," Lucy answered, seating herself upon an ottoman. "Here I am your humble servant to command what orders for your slave, most noble Isabel of Leicester. You have but to speak and I obey."

"Do be sensible Lucy and let mamma know that Isabel has come," said Ada reprovingly.

"I go," answered Lucy with mock gravity, "to usher my illustrious mother to the presence of the noble Isabel of Leicester."

"Oh! Lucy, just the same nonsensical," laughed Isabel.

"Alas, I fear that it will be the same to the end of the chapter," sighed the incorrigible Lucy as she left the room. She soon returned bringing the other members of the family with her, and Isabel received a very warm welcome. She could not help shedding tears of happiness and gratitude, when Mrs. Mornington embracing her said, "ever look upon this as your home dear child, whenever you like to come you will always find us glad to see you," and Mr. Mornington added in his kindly tone "yes, yes, always remember Isabel my dear, that while I have a roof over my head, you have still a home, and kind friends to welcome you."

On being conducted to her room, she found the best was

given her as of old; it was evident that her altered circumstances made no difference at Eastwood.

Happy days were these which Isabel spent with her dearest friends. Bob's party went off with great *eclat*, and the perfect success of the Xmas trees was owing to Isabel's tasteful arrangement.

The Ashtons arrived on New Year's Eve, for Ada was to be married on twelfth day. Lady Ashton was very much surprised to find how very partial the Morningtons were to Isabel, they consulted her on all occasions, and her advice was almost invariably taken. This annoyed Lady Ashton extremely, and she often succeeded in vexing her, and making her feel very uncomfortable. But Lady Ashton's disagreeable behaviour did not annoy Isabel so much as at Ashton Park. Here among her best friends, she could even think of herself as a governess without experiencing the same degree of mortification as formerly, but she was still very sensitive upon that point.

Lady Ashton had noticed that her nephew, The Honorable Arthur Barrington was very attentive to Miss Leicester, this raised her ire, and she was determined to prevent it—she resolved to put a stop to it, so seeing him seated next Isabel at dinner, she asked her across the table how her little pupils were when she left them, and if Mrs. Arlington had granted extra holidays, as she could scarcely get back by the end of the usual Xmas vacation."

Isabel grew scarlet as she replied "that they were quite well when she left them, and that she did not return until the first of February."

Lady Ashton was gratified to see that she was successful so far. Isabel was no longer the same attentive listener to all

Arthur's stories of marvellous adventures, (for she was both hurt and angry, as the question was evidently intended to annoy—for as Emily had come to Eastwood with the Ashtons, Lady Ashton had later intelligence from Elm Grove than she could possibly give) and Arthur finding her pre-occupied, transferred his attention to Mabel Ainsley, so that Isabel was left to the mercy of a queer old gentleman who sat next her on the other side, who was exceedingly deaf, and stuttered dreadfully. Nor did Lady Ashton's evident satis-faction tend to make her feel more at ease, so that she was heartily glad when this to her most tedious dinner was over. But she had a worse attack to endure, for when the ladies reached the drawing-room, Lady Ashton said in the most annoying tone, "I should not have mentioned your pupils if I had had any idea that you would have been so painfully affected by my doing so, at the same time rest assured my dear Miss Leicester—."

"Pray don't mention it Lady Ashton," replied Isabel coldly, "any apology is quite unnecessary."

"You mistake my meaning Miss Leicester," replied Lady Ashton stiffly, "I am not aware of having anything to apologize for," she added with a contemptuous little laugh, "I was about to say" she continued, "that the sooner you over-come this feeling the better. You ought not to be ashamed of earning an honest living—."

"Nor am I ashamed of it," replied Isabel with dignity, "at least I hope not."

"I am glad that you qualify your denial, as your crimson cheeks both now and during dinner are ample proof that I am right. But (as I was about to say, when you interrupted me so rudely) from my observations, I thought it high time that Mr. Barrington should be reminded of your position, as I know that his father would never allow him to marry a governess, of course it is no disgrace to be a governess, still, it is not from that class of persons that Arthur should choose a wife."

"I'm afraid that you have taken unnecessary trouble, Lady Ashton," returned Isabel, "I am convinced that my position is of no consequence to Mr. Barrington, any more than his is to me. I assure you that you have made a great mistake."

"It is nonsense for a girl in your circumstances to pretend such indifference, I am not deceived, I know that you would be only too glad to make such a match, and he is just foolish enough to take a fancy to a pretty face. But I warn you not to encourage him, as it will only end in misery to you both, as Lord Barrington would never consent."

"Really, Lady Ashton, I do not know what right you have to insult me in this manner, I cannot permit it," said Isabel, and then with dignified composure she crossed the room to Ada, who was scarcely less annoyed than herself, at Lady Ashton's unprovoked attack.

This little scene had afforded no little amusement to the party generally, tho' all agreed that it was too bad of Lady Ashton, and very ill-natured.

Lady Ashton, however, had miscalculated the effect of the course she had pursued, for Arthur Barrington was annoyed at her interference, and being really good-natured he was even more than ever attentive to Isabel, and endeavored as much as possible to atone for his aunt's disagreeable behaviour, while Isabel (being convinced that Lady Ashton had nothing to warrant her conjecture, but her own surmises,) made no alteration in her manners. She found him a very agreeable companion, and imagined that he too found her society pleasant, as indeed he did, beautiful, accomplished, and good-natured, how could she be otherwise than attractive. But Lady Ashton's chagrin knew no bounds, and she told Isabel that she should certainly let Mrs. Arlington know how very unfit a person she was to have the care of her daughters. She had always been surprised at her having such a very young person, but she had heard that it was out of charity, but there was such a thing as carrying that much abused virtue too far.

Stooping lower over her tatting, Isabel only smiled at the harmless threat, for whatever her failings might be, Mrs. Arlington was not over ready to believe evil of any one, and seldom did so without due cause. Moreover, she was not easily influenced by others, and her decisions were usually just. But the hot blood suffused her cheeks as Lady Ashton concluded. Fortunately Lucy entered the room, and then her ladyship was or appeared to be deeply engaged with her book, as having before been worsted in a combat of sharp speeches with that young lady, she by no means wished for a renewal of hostilities.

Isabel was invariably made low spirited by one of Lady Ashton's ill-natured attacks, especially so to-day, as the insults she had received were particularly painful, being both unfeeling and uncalled for. However, upon retiring to her own room at night, she found upon the dressing table a letter, the contents of which soon dispersed all gloomy thoughts, and Lady Ashton's rudeness was quite forgotten.

Louis, her own dear Louis, wrote that he would return in the early spring. My uncle he said, has or is about to purchase for me a practice in H——, so that I trust dearest, the period of your teaching will not be of long duration, as there will then be no cause to delay our union. I already in perspective, seem to see you my own dearest, presiding over my bright fireside in H——, the joy of my heart, and the good angel of my home.

I trust that you have made no arrangement with Mrs. Arlington but such as can easily terminate upon a short notice. I would not advise your taking any steps at present, as my uncle does not say positively that the purchase is absolutely made. But at all events you may depend upon seeing me in the early spring, as I have his orders to return.

The darkest hour is just before dawn. She had been so truly wretched an hour ago, and now how radiantly happy she was. Ah, with what sweet visions of a bright unclouded future did she fall asleep, to dream of her loved one far away, soon to be distant no longer.

When Isabel descended to the breakfast-room next morning, she looked so bright and happy, that Lady Ashton could account for it in no other way than that Arthur had proposed, and that she had accepted him, so she taxed him with it accordingly. Arthur was excessively amused, and so archly evaded giving a direct answer, that she became the more convinced of the truth of her own surmises, and grew so wrathy that Arthur fearing that in her anger she might annoy Miss Leicester, at length assured her that she need be under no apprehension, as nothing was farther from his thoughts.

CHAPTER VII

"Oh, Isabel, mama says I may stay until the first, and then we can return together, won't that be charming," said Emily, as she came into Isabel's room on the following day, holding an open letter in her hand. "You can't think how glad I am to escape the escort of that tiresome Lady Ashton."

"I certainly should not imagine that she would make a very pleasant travelling companion," returned Isabel, laughing. "Don't mention it pray," exclaimed Emily, "you have no idea what I endured coming down. Poor Charles, he must have been almost worried to death, she is such a horrid tease, and the old gentleman too, is an awful fidget. I think Arthur Barrington knew what he was about, when he refused to be of our party, and went on by express. Talking of Lady Ashton, how abominably she behaves to you. I was saying so to Harry the other day, and he really seemed quite hurt about it. He said that he saw what she was at the other day at dinner, and was very much annoyed. Then I told him that was nothing to what took place afterwards, and related what she said to you in the drawing room."

"Oh, Emily, how could you," exclaimed Isabel.

"Ah now don't be cross with me, Isabel, darling. I really couldn't resist, it was so supremely absurd. Do you know, that that little goose, Ada, cried her eyes out about it that night, and then in again next morning." "I know that Ada was very much hurt at Lady Ashton's rudeness," replied Isabel.

"I'm sure that I was as angry and annoyed as any of them, but for the life of me I can't help laughing whenever I think of it. But confess now, Isabel, are you not desperately in love with Arthur Barrington—come tell the truth."

"Well, the truth is, no, most decidedly not," Isabel answered, laughing.

"Ah, now, I'm quite disappointed, for I had made up my mind to that match, if only to aggravate Lady Ashton. She has no influence in that quarter, as anyone may see; and he is so decidedly 'smitten.'"

"What nonsense you talk, Emily."

"It is not nonsense. I assure you that I mean what I say. Ah, my dear, you had better consider the matter. Second thoughts, you know, are sometimes best. He is a very nice fellow, and his father is immensely rich. You can have him if you choose: I am sharp enough to see that."

"But then you see I don't choose," returned Isabel, much amused. "Besides, I think that you are quite mistaken."

"Oh, you silly Isabel, how can you be so provokingly stupid? By the bye, what a little namby-pamby thing that Mabel Ainsley is. What Lucy can see in her to like, passes my comprehension."

"I presume it must be because Lucy is so different, and then Mabel is so pliant, which no doubt suits, as Lucy is fond of taking the lead."

"They say that likes go by contraries; but as far as my observations go, it is seldom the case," observed Emily.

"A similarity of tastes and ideas is usually more attractive; but then, 'novelty's charming,' you know," responded Isabel.

"I do wish that we could get up a fancy ball—a private masquerade, you know. I was speaking to Ada and Lucy about it last night. I said that I would be night, and Lucy thought you ought to be morning."

"I hope they will give up the idea, as I really could not take part in it," interrupted Isabel.

"Why not—what harm could there be? What makes you so fastidious, Isabel?"

"It is not that, dear Emily;" but I have very painful associations connected with a private masquerade, the only one that I ever went to. That night poor papa received the sad news of his failure; and in the midst of that gay scene, I received a summons to return, as my papa was alarmingly ill, and scarcely expected to live through the night. He never recovered, though he lingered for some weeks afterwards. Can you wonder then, dear Emily, that even the idea of such a thing is painful in the extreme?"

"I'm very sorry that I proposed it," returned Emily, much concerned. "I will tell Ada what you say, and we will get up some other amusement: so don't think any more about it, dear;" and giving Isabel a hasty kiss, she left her.

The sixth was a bright, cloudless day—the dazzling whiteness of the frozen snow, and the deep blue of the sky, forming a beautiful contrast. The weather was cold, not intensely so, and the trees looked splendid, as their ice-covered boughs glistened and sparkled in the sunlight; and the merry jingle of the sleigh-bells was quite enlivening. The wedding was quite a grand affair, and passed off with great *eclat.*

Charles and Ada were to travel for three weeks, and then join the Ashtons and Morningtons at Boston, and proceed to the old country together.

The Ashtons left Eastwood shortly after the wedding, to prepare for a long absence from the Park; and from the time of Lady Ashton's departure, Isabel's visit was one of uninterrupted enjoyment. She became so cheerful and animated, that Emily declared they positively wouldn't know her again at Elm Grove.

Harry was to remain at W—, to read up for the examination. He had tried very hard to prevail upon his father to let him enter Mr. Arlington's office, as in that way he could get on much better, he said, as he would see a great deal of law business, and he could easily read up in the evenings.

But his father only laughed. "Love-making would play the dickens with the studies. You would be poring over your book, without knowing that it was upside down. No, no. After you have 'passed,' you shall travel for a year; and then I believe that I shall be able to get you a partnership in H— with my old school-fellow, Harding, who is a very clever lawyer, and stands very high in his profession."

"But will you allow me sufficient to enable me to marry and take my wife with me?" asked Harry.

"Upon my word! that is a modest request," replied his father.

Harry laughed.

"When I was young, young men expected to make their way in the world a little before they talked of marrying," continued Mr. Mornington; but you ask me as coolly as possible to give you enough to enable you and your wife to travel, before you go into business at all, which I think is pretty brassy. I wonder what my father would have thought if I had made such a request. I honestly believe he would have thrashed me. But as I said, things are different now-a-days." Harry grew very red during this harangue, but wisely kept silent.

"Now, I'll tell you what my father did. He called me into his study one morning. 'How old are you?' he asked. 'Fifteen, sir,' I replied proudly. 'Old enough to be better,' he retorted. 'Well, sir, as you are fifteen, I consider that you are old enough to earn your own living. I have procured you a situation in a wholesale grocery, where you will get a hundred dollars a year. Now, as you will be away from home (for the firm is in Washington), I will pay your board for the first year. After that, you will get a rise in your salary; and from that time, you will have to depend upon your own exertions, as I shall not help you any more. If you are honest and steady, you get on. But if you will get into scrapes, don't expect me to help you out." "Yes, sir," resumed Mr. Mornington, "that was the way I began the world; and by the time I was twenty-three (your age, Harry), I had acquired a good position in the firm, and a promise of a future partnership. What do you think of that?"

"I think that if you had started me in the same manner, when I was fifteen, that I should have done the same," replied Harry, with spirit.

"Then you think that you can't be blamed justly?"

"No, sir," returned Harry, respectfully.

"Well, I suppose that it has been all my own doing," resumed Mr. Mornington. "But seriously, Harry, do you wish to give up law and become one of the firm? Speak out, boy, there is no good in taking up a thing if you have no heart for it."

"You mistake me altogether," interposed Harry, hastily. "I have not the least wish to give up the law."

"So let it be then. And I agree to your request—provided that you 'pass' within a year."

"All right—thanks," returned Harry, thinking that he had made a capital arrangement.

"I suppose," added his father, "that you will have to take the girls to Elm Grove."

"Unless it interferes with the bargain," Harry began—

"Ha, ha!" laughed Mr. Mornington. "You will make a good lawyer yet, I believe."

"I hope so," responded Harry, lighting his cigar.

On the first of February, they all set out for Boston, according to the previous arrangement. On their arrival in that city, they found that Charles and Ada had been there some days. Charles had received a telegram, saying that the elder Ashtons would only get there an hour or so before the steamer left.

The girls were delighted at this intelligence, as now there was nothing to mar the happiness of the party during the few days that they would spend together. Ada and Isabel were inseparable, and it was astonishing how much Lucy and Emily had to say. Charles and Harry discussed their future plans. Mr. Mornington had a great many people to see, and a great deal of business to attend to, so that he was closely occupied, and had scarcely a word for any one during meals, which was the only time he was with them. And Mrs. Mornington's happiness seemed to consist in seeing the young people enjoy themselves.

After the arrival of Sir John and Lady Ashton, with Miss Crosse and Louisa, they all went on board the steamer; and when they had seen them comfortably settled, Emily, Harry and Isabel, returned to the hotel, and the next morning continued their journey to Elm Grove, where Mr. Mornington had stipulated that Harry should stay no more than three weeks—or it would interfere with the bargain.

CHAPTER VIII

The Arlingtons had a grand ball in honor of Miss Arlington's twenty-first birthday, which Rose said wasn't fair, as Everard didn't have one on his. Mrs. Arlington, always celebrated for the taste and elegance displayed at her parties, has almost surpassed all former occasions in the magnificent arrangement of everything.

Isabel wore a plain white dress, and jet ornaments. A single flower adorned her hair; and the usual, rather sad expression of her countenance, was exchanged for one of greater animation. The excitement of the occasion had given an unwonted glow to her cheeks. She did, indeed, look lovely, as she stood engaged in lively conversation with Emily, while they were waiting in the drawing-room to receive the guests; and so Everard thought, who stood talking with his father, while his eyes rested admiringly upon Isabel's sweet face.

After the greater part of the guests had arrived, and the dancing fairly commenced, Isabel, who had been waltzing, returned to the drawing-room. She was scarcely seated, when, to her utter amazement, she saw Louis Taschereau enter. Oh, how her heart throbbed at the unexpected meeting! Here was Louis, her own Louis, actually in the room. It was annoying, that after being parted so long, they should first meet in a crowded ball-room.—Never mind; she was only too glad to have him there. He looked so well, so bright and happy, as he made his way through the crowd, with the proud bearing and haughty mien in which she delighted. How long would it be before he reached her?—Oh, that the room were smaller, or that she had been nearer the door. It seemed an age while he was shaking hands with Mrs. Arlington. But who is that pretty girl on his arm? Could it be his cousin Marie? He has taken her to a seat, and is moving down the room. The hot blood rushed to her cheeks. Someone asked her to dance. "Oh, not yet," she replied, scarcely heeding who it was that asked her. Louis sees her, and is coming towards her. How her heart bounded, her joy and happiness was so great. She hid her glowing face behind her fan, to conceal her confusion. Another moment and he was by her side, greeting her cordially. "Oh, Louis," and she smiled upon him, O so sweetly. "You did not expect to see me to-night," he said, looking very contented and triumphant. But there was something in the expression of his face which she did not like—something that seemed to freeze up all the warmth of her feelings in an instant. Was it that he thought she was too ready to show what she felt, with so many present who might observe any unusual degree of pleasure on her part. Oh, surely not, for she had been so careful—as careful as it was in human nature to be.

"Was that your cousin," she asked, "that you brought with you?"

"No! that—is—my wife—" he said, with a look of triumph.

"Your wife! Why, what do you mean?" she inquired, thinking he was jesting.

"Just what I say," he replied. Then, with insufferable

insolence, he hissed in her ear, "Louis Taschereau never forgives."

"Indeed," she answered, assuming an air of indifference that surprised even herself; for she had felt the hot, indignant blood, coursing through her veins.

"Really," he said, with cool effrontery, "that assumption of indifference is sublime. But I am not deceived," he continued, with a scornful laugh; "my revenge is most complete, my plans have been entirely successful," and making her a low bow, he retired. And Isabel was left to her own thoughts. But this would not do; she must not—dare not—think; she must have excitement until she could be quite alone. Fortunately, Harry now claimed her as his partner. "Oh, Harry," she said, "I am so tired of sitting here."

"Why, I asked you for the last dance, and you wouldn't come," answered Harry, laughing.

"I didn't think it would have lasted so long," she returned.

"Do you know that Louis is here?" he inquired.

"Yes."

"Don't you think his wife pretty?"

"Very."

Harry knew that Louis had always been a favorite with Isabel, but the remotest idea of the real state of the case never for a moment occured to him.

When the dance was over, they went out on the glass extension room. Presently Harry said abruptly:

"Isabel, I really thought that you would have been Mrs. Taschereau."

"Harry!"

"I did, indeed."

"Harry, don't," she said imploringly.

Just then Everard and Emily came in, and at the next dance they exchanged partners. As they passed under the hall lamp, Everard remarked the extreme palor of her countenance. "You are ill, Miss Leicester," he said. You should not have remained so long in that cold place. Let me get you a glass of wine."

"Oh no, thanks. I shall soon get warm with dancing."

"I don't think that you should attempt this galop. You look too ill; indeed you do."

"I intend to dance it, Mr. Arlington; but if you do not wish too, I can have another partner." Everard looked so sad and reproachful as she said this, that she felt sorry for the hasty words. She knew they had been harsh, and he had said nothing but what was kind—nothing to deserve anything so severe. But then she dare not sit during a single dance; she could not, would not, rest a moment. She was making a great effort to 'keep up,' and it was only by a continual struggle that she could succeed. However, Everard had no more cause for uneasiness on account of her looking ill, as they had scarcely entered the ball-room before her brilliant color had returned. Isabel was decidedly the belle of the evening; and for this, Grace Arlington never forgave her. Everard saw that Isabel's gaiety was assumed, and he would have given much to know the cause. Harry was not so keen an observer, and only thought how much she was enjoying herself, and how much he had been mistaken in thinking that she cared anything about Louis.

Oh the weary, weary length of that dreadful evening. Isabel thought that it would never end. But she kept up splendidly. Once she unexpectedly found Louis her *vis a vis*—then came the master-piece of the evening. She looked superb, as with graceful dignity she glided through the quadrille. She avoided touching his hand, except when it was inevitable; but she did it so naturally, that to others it did not appear premeditated. He spoke to her, but she passed on as though she did not hear. Once again, before the dance was ended, he ventured to address her; but she replied with grave dignity, "We must meet as strangers: henceforth I shall not know you, Dr. Taschereau."

Louis foamed with rage at the cool contempt conveyed in these words. He ground his teeth, and swore to be revenged. At last the guests all departed, and Harry too had taken leave (for as this was his last day at Elm Grove, he was going by the three o'clock train to keep his promise, for Harry was very strict, and would not have remained another day on any pretext). Then Isabel had to listen to the praises bestowed on her by all the Arlington family, who complimented her upon the sensation she had made, and to force herself to join in an animated conversation regarding the events of the evening; so that she was truly glad when Mr. Arlington dismissed the 'conclave,' saying that they could discuss the party next day.

When Isabel gained her own room, and sat down to think of her trouble, she began to realize the full extent of her misery. She had scarcely known 'till now, how much his love had supported her through all her trials; or how the thought of one day being his, had softened the ills she had been called upon to endure since her father's death. Now she must think of him no more—he was hers no longer. But worse than this, was the pain and grief of knowing that he was unworthy of the love and admiration that she had bestowed upon him. She knew that he was proud, passionate and exacting, yet she loved him; for these very characteristics, mingled as they were with more endearing qualities, had a peculiar charm for her. How happy she had been to feel that he loved her; and oh! the pain, the agony, of knowing that he did so no longer. Why, why had he written that letter? Oh it was cruel, cruel. And then to think that it had all been planned, premeditated, with the express design of making her suffer more acutely, was bitter in the extreme. To lose his love was misery; but to know that he was deceitful, cruel and revengeful, was agony beyond endurance. She did not weep: her grief was too stony for tears. "Oh, Louis, Louis," she moaned in her agony, "what have I done, to deserve such cruel treatment?" She leaned her head upon her arm, and pressed her hand upon her throbbing temples, for the tumult of her thoughts became intolerable. She pictured to herself Louis, as she loved to see him; old scenes recurred to her mind, and the days when she had been so happy in his love—nor had a wish beyond. Even this very night, how inexpressibly happy had it made her to see him in the room. And oh, to have all her dreams of happiness crushed in a moment. Again she thought how different it might have been had he been faithful and true; but he was false—he did not love her, and what had she to live for now? A sense of oppression, which almost amounted to suffocation, distressed her, until at length a fearful sensation of choking forced her to rise to get some water; but ere she could do so, a crimson stream flowed from her mouth, down her white dress, and she fell upon the floor.

Clotilda Jennings

CHAPTER IX

The daylight was streaming in at the window when Emily awoke, and lay thinking of the party, and rejoicing in her kind little heart that Isabel had been so happy, and had enjoyed herself so much. Then she sighed as she thought Harry was gone, but smiled again at the bright prospect she had in view, for Harry had imparted to her the nice arrangement that he had made with his father, and she did so love the idea of travelling for a year. Then again she heaved a little sigh, and hoped he would not overwork himself; but there was no cause for uneasiness on that score, for Harry was too much accustomed to take things easy, and too wise to work himself to death: and Emmy was content to believe this.

But she was that sociable disposition, that she could not half enjoy anything unless she could get some one to sympathise with her. She did so long to tell her news. Late as was the hour when the party broke up, she wanted to tell Isabel; but Isabel had refused their accustomed chat, saying that it was too late, and that Mrs. Arlington would be vexed.

Then she wondered if Isabel was awake, she did so long to tell her about the year's travelling. She thought she would go and see. So she got up very quietly, partially dressed, and then threw on her dressing gown, and ran up to Isabel's room; but finding the door locked, she rattled the handle slightly, and called through the key-hole, "Isabel! Isabel! are you awake? open the door." Then as she drew back, something attracted her sight, and impelled her to apply her eye to the said key-hole. She did so; and horrified beyond description at what she beheld, she shrieked aloud with terror. Her frantic cries brought her father, mother, Everard, and several of the servants, to the rescue.

"Open the door! oh, open the door!" was all that she could say, wringing her hands in anguish, and pointing to it.

"Speak, child," said her father, "what is the matter?"

But she only cried more wildly, "open the door! open the door!" without attempting to explain. But Everard, with his firm, quiet manner, and reassuring tone, calmed her almost instantly.

Mrs. Arlington did as Emily had done before her. "There is something wrong," she exclaimed, "we must get the door open."

The united efforts of Everard and his father forced the door, and a more distressing sight can scarcely be imagined than that they beheld. Stretched on the floor lay Isabel, in her ball dress, the blood pouring from her mouth in a crimson stream. As soon as Everard saw this, he waited for no more, but hastened to the stable, and was soon on the road, dashing at a reckless pace, towards Dr. Heathfield's. Mrs. Arlington quietly desired Norris to remove the children, who, alarmed by Emily's cries, had crowded into the room, along with the servants. Emily also was dismissed; and ordering two of the servants to remain, she told the rest to retire, and to send Norris back again. She then turned her attention to the suffering girl, whose face wore an expression of ineffable agony; but she was at a loss how to proceed, not knowing what ought to be done, and fearing that she might do harm by injudicious treatment. In less time than could have been imagined, Everard returned with the doctor, who had great difficulty in stopping the bleeding. She had broken a blood vessel, he said, and was in a very dangerous state. He ordered perfect quiet, as the least excitement would cause a return of the bleeding, and then nothing could save her. He questioned very sharply as to what had happened, and gave as his opinion that it had been caused by some great shock, and violent emotion struggled with and suppressed, by undue excitement.

Mrs. Arlington repudiated the notion, and protested against such an assumption, saying "that Miss Leicester appeared quite well when she retired to rest."

"These things do not happen without cause, madam," returned the doctor; "therefore in all probability something has occurred of which you know nothing."

"I am convinced that you are mistaken, Dr. Heathfield; but I will take care that your orders are strictly attended to. No one but myself and Norris shall be allowed in the room. You have no doubt of her ultimate recovery, I trust," she added.

"I couldn't pretend to give an opinion at present; I can only tell you that she is in a most precarious state," he replied gravely. "Everything depends upon the prevention of the hemorrhage, a return of which would be certain death. At the same time, that is not all that we have to fear."

For a long time Isabel hovered between life and death, scarcely conscious of what was passing around her. Day after day the children would linger on the stairs, whenever the doctor came, to hear his account of Miss Leicester. But he only shook his head, and said "he could not have them there. Their governess was very ill, and they must be very good children." Then they would return to the school-room, and spend, as best they might, these joyless holidays.

At last the longed for answer came—"She was certainly better," and they were delighted beyond measure; but their joy was considerably damped, when he told them that they could not be permitted to see her for some time yet.

Isabel's recovery was very slow, though every care and attention was bestowed upon her, and each vied with the other in showing kindness to the orphan girl. Still Isabel felt her lonely, dependent condition, acutely. Life seemed a dreary, cheerless existence; and she experienced a shrinking from the future which seemed to be before her, which was at times almost insupportable. She longed to be at rest. The prostration and langour, both mental and bodily, that accompanied this depression, was so great as to seriously retard her recovery, and almost baffled the doctor's skill. She would lie for hours without speaking or moving, apparently asleep, but only in a sort of waking dream. She took no interest in anything, and appeared quite incapable of making any effort to overcome this apathy. Emily tried her best to amuse her; but after taking pains to relate everything that she thought of interest that had occurred, Isabel would smile and thank her, in a way that proved she had not been listening. Thus week after week of her convalescence passed, while, to the doctor's surprise and disappointment, she made no further progress. After visiting his patient one afternoon, he requested a few moments' conversation with Mrs. Arlington. "My dear madam," he said, when that lady had led the way into the morning-room, "has Miss Leicester no friends, with whom she could spend a few weeks? for if she is allowed to remain in this lethargic state, she will inevitably sink. An entire change of air and scene is absolutely necessary. She requires something to rouse her in a gentle way, without excitement."

"She has friends, I believe; but really, I know so little about them, that any arrangement of that sort is out of the question. All those I do know, are at present in Europe," returned Mrs. Arlington. "But we are anxious to do everything in our power to promote her recovery. If you can suggest anything, I shall be most happy to carry out your plans. I proposed her going to the sea-side, but she wouldn't hear of it, and said that she hoped she should not trouble us much longer. I remonstrated, but to no purpose—she persisted that it was utterly impossible."

"That was the very thing I was going to suggest," returned the doctor; "but I trusted that the proposal would have met with a better reception. But if you will allow me, I think I might persuade her to accompany the children, as if on their account. Have I your permission to do so?"

"Full permission to make any arrangements that you think beneficial, doctor," replied Mrs. Arlington.

Doctor Heathfield went back to his patient. He found her alone. "What do you think of making a start to the sea-side? I think it would do you good."

"Oh, indeed I could not," returned Isabel languidly. "Mrs. Arlington is very kind, but it is quite impossible."

"Don't decide so hastily," replied Dr. Heathfield, taking a seat by her side.

"A thing which is impossible, requires no consideration."

"But I am convinced that it is not impossible," he urged, "and by obliging others, you will also benefit yourself; it is such a very small thing that is required of you, just to accompany the children to D—for a few weeks. Indeed I think that you can scarcely refuse after all the kindness that you have received during your long illness."

"I am extremely sorry to have caused so much trouble, but I assure you that I am not ungrateful."

"It don't seem like it when you won't do what little you might to please," returned the doctor.

"Don't say will not," Dr. Heathfield.

"Ay but I must say will not, and excuse me when I add, that you greatly mistake your duty to give way to this apathy, and thus retard your recovery," he said kindly. "I do not seek to fathom your trouble, but I do know that it was excessive mental anguish that caused you to break a blood-vessel, and I would remind you that this is not the right way to brood over and nurse your grief, refusing to make any effort to do your duty.

"I know it is wrong faltered Isabel with quivering lips, but I cannot take an interest in anything or find comfort, save in the thought of early death."

"But that is from the morbid state of mind induced by weakness."

Isabel shook her head.

"And will pass off as you get stronger," he continued.

"I shall never be strong again," she said.

"Pooh, nonsense, I can't have you talk in that way, if you only make an effort and go with the children to D—, I think you will soon alter your opinion."

"Please don't say any more, my head aches dreadfully," pleaded Isabel.

"One moment and I have done," he said, "I fear that you forget your position here, the family have behaved to you with the greatest generosity, but still you must be aware that they would not continue to keep an invalid governess, and as I understand that you are entirely dependant upon your own exertions, you must see the necessity of trying the benefit of sea air, when you have the opportunity, do not take it unkindly that I have used such freedom in pressing this matter, think over it quietly, and to-morrow let me know what answer I am to give Mrs. Arlington." Then he took his leave, and his kind heart smote him, for he heard the smothered sobs of his fair patient.

CHAPTER X

Mrs. Arlington never for a moment suspected the way in which Dr. Heathfield would induce Isabel to accede to his plans. In justice to her it must be said, that had she known it, she would if possible have prevented it. But in the end perhaps it was better for Isabel that she did not, though the reflections to which his remarks gave rise, were extremely painful. It needed not these cruel hints to remind her of that which had scarcely ever been absent from her thoughts since her father's death, and she shed very bitter tears, even after she retired to rest she could but weep over her unhappy lot far into the night, until at length the bright moonlight streaming in at the window, reminded her of one above, who doeth all things well, and she resolved to try and do her duty according to His appointment, however trying she might find it, trusting that as her need was, so would strength be given.

She saw now why she had not been allowed to die according to her wish, even because her work was not yet accomplished. How willingly and with what pleasure had the children received what she had taught them regarding religion; how eagerly had they listened when she had explained the scriptures; with what different feelings did they now regard the sabbath as a day of holy rest, and prayer, and praise, instead of a day of weariness, dreaded and hated. Did she not remember how shocked she had been, when

Clotilda Jennings

Amy said, that she liked all the days except sundays, and the others had expressed the same. And oh, how glad and thankful she felt when Amy not long since, one sunday afternoon had clasped her arms round her neck, and exclaimed that she liked Miss Leicester's sundays very much. All this she had been able to do through divine blessing upon her endeavors to benefit the children, and would she leave them when her work had only just begun? No, no, how wrong and selfish had she been, if all joy and happiness had fled, she still had her work before her—her duty to perform. With such thoughts as these, her tears became less bitter. Soft tear of quiet resignation followed the bitter rebellious ones she had shed so abundantly, and she resolved by steady abnegation of self, to forget the past (as much as might be) in the business and duties of the present. Then with a prayer for strength to keep this resolution, and patience to wait, and work until such time as rest should be vouchsafed her, she fell asleep.

With a severe headache, and extremely weak from the trying night she had past, Isabel waited for the doctor next day, though she had determined to give him a favorable answer, she wondered much how she could go, when she felt almost unable to raise her hand to her head. She was feverish and restless, very anxious for his arrival, yet dreading it, for it seemed as though she were about by her own act, to put an end to these quiet days of rest, and dreamy reverie, which she fain would prolong.

However, when Dr. Heathfield came, she managed to return his greeting with some degree of cheerfulness.

"I trust you feel better to-day," he said.

"No, rather worse, the dose you administered was anti-narcotic I assure you, but I have decided to accede to Mrs.

Arlington's wishes. I will do my utmost for the children, but I fear that will be very little," and she smiled faintly from her pillow.

"Pooh, nonsense, you are not to teach at present, we all know you can't do that," returned the doctor cheerfully, "what good would the poor children get if they were cooped up in a school-room all day, time enough for that when they come home again." Dr. Heathfield began to fear that the dose had been too strong, when he felt the feverish pulse. "You must be very quiet to-day, promise me that you will not worry yourself," he said, "I shall tell Mrs. Arlington not to let the girls tease you."

"They never tease me." replied Isabel hastily.

"Oh they don't, well that is fortunate," he answered, preparing some mysterious compound that he had taken from his pocket, "now if you take this" he continued, presenting the mixture, "and then take a nice little sleep, you will feel much better by the afternoon, and then if Miss Emily would read to you, it would be better than talking."

"I'm afraid your patient is not so well to-day doctor," said Mrs. Arlington coming in, "she seems feverish this morning."

"Oh, she has been tormenting herself, thinking that she had to teach while at D—, but I think if you keep her quiet, this feverishness will soon subside, and she is going with the children to D—like a good sensible girl," replied the doctor.

"I am very glad that you have come to that decision Isabel, as I should not think of sending the children without you," (no more she would) said Mrs. Arlington, keeping up the farce that she was the obliged party. "Emily and Norris go with you, so that you have no cause for anxiety, dear," she added, laying her cool hand upon Isabel's hot forehead.

"Is your head very bad," inquired the doctor, pulling down the blind. Then as Isabel assented, he went on, "if you were to send the quiet one, (Alice I think you call her) to bathe her temples with a little lotion it would be as well."

"I think it should be Norris, I don't like to trust the children," Mrs. Arlington began.

"You may trust Alice," interrupted Isabel.

"Very well," returned Mrs. Arlington smiling, "then Alice it shall be."

Within a week, everything was arranged for their departure, Everard was to escort them to D—and see them comfortably settled, and then proceed to H—College. The morning they were to start, Isabel joined them at the early school-room breakfast. This was the first time that Everard had seen her since her illness, and he was inexpressibly shocked at her appearance, and remonstrated with his mother, saying, that Miss Leicester was not in a fit state to travel.

"My dear Everard, I am acting entirely under the the doctor's orders."

"Nevertheless it is cruel," he replied gravely.

"My dear son what can I do, Dr. Heathfield says that it is absolutely necessary."

"It will kill her, that is my opinion of the matter." he answered "why she can scarcely stand, I had no idea she was so awfully weak."

"But what can I do," persisted Mrs. Arlington.

"Wait until she gets a little stronger," urged Everard.

"But the doctor assures me, that she will inevitable sink, if allowed to remain in the same low spirited state."

"Why did you not have her among the rest, and then probably she might not have got so low. It is dreadful to see any one so fearfully weak," he added in a tone of grave commiseration.

"I don't wonder at your being shocked at her altered appearance, but you should not blame those who have had the care of her, without due consideration. I assure you that she has had every attention," said Mrs. Arlington reproachfully.

"I don't wish to blame any one," returned Everard coloring, "surely not you dear mother."

"I am glad to hear it," she answered, in a somewhat injured tone. "I was sure that it only required a moment's thought to convince you, that however painful a state Miss Leicester may be in, it has been brought about by circumstances over which we have no control."

Everard looked perseveringly out of the window. And his mother continued "it was at her own request that she remained so secluded. But it must not be, we have listened to her entreaties too long already, now others must act for her in the way they think best."

"Then it is not her wish to go," observed Everard.

"Certainly not, but the doctor almost insists upon it."

"Kill or cure as I take it," he returned.

"I fear that is too near the truth, unfortunately," replied his mother."

"Everard remained silent, and Mrs. Arlington saying that the carriage would be round shortly, quitted the room. Then he returned to the school-room, to find Isabel fainting upon the sofa and Emily bending over her in helpless despair, Amy crying, and Alice emptying the contents of a scent bottle over Isabel, and Rose spilling the smelling salts almost into her mouth, in her anxiety to cram it to her nose. This quaint mode of treatment had the desired effect, for Isabel with a great sigh opened her eyes, and asked what was the matter. Dr. Heathfield arrived soon after this, and ordered Miss Leicester back to her room for a few hours rest, so that they were forced to wait for the next train.

"She ought not to have come down to breakfast," he said, "let her have lunch in her own room, and remain there until everything is quite ready, then let her go straight to the carriage after the rest are seated, it must be managed quietly or it cannot be done." Then he called Everard aside, and cautioned him, "it is a hazardous thing to move her at all, and requires very nice management," he said.

"It should not be attempted," returned Everard coldly, "she is only fit to be in bed."

"The doctor smiled incredulously, keep her there and you would soon finish her, and she would be only too content to do it."

"You are severe Dr. Heathfield," said Everard stiffly.

"Come, Come, Everard don't get angry, you think me a brute

no doubt. But if she remains here she will die, if she goes away she may recover. Now you have my honest opinion."

"It seems to me little short of murder, to start her off in this state," returned Everard."

"Upon my word, who is severe now Mr. Everard," retorted the doctor. I don't attempt to deny that moving her may be fatal, if not judiciously managed But if carefully and properly done, I am very sanguine as to the result.

"That is a nice way of getting out of a scrape, I must say," "Oh a very nice way indeed," said Dr. Heathfield laughing. "I will come in again about one," he added addressing Mrs. Arlington, "and if I have time, I will go down to the station and see them off."

"Oh, if you could doctor, it would be such a satisfaction to know that you were with them," Mrs. Arlington answered.

Everard could not bring himself to see it in the same light as the doctor, but as her going seemed inevitable, he was glad that he was to have the charge of her. A little before one the doctor returned, but only to see that all was right. "He was so very busy," he said, "but had no doubt that Mr. Everard would manage very well. He could not possibly go down to the station, he had to set a man's leg two miles off in quite another direction. Everard's face was a picture, as the doctor so kindly expressed the belief that he would manage very well. Emily was so convulsed with laughter at the sight, that she was forced to stuff her handkerchief into her mouth to conceal her mirth. Everard managed everything so nicely during the journey, that Isabel never knew that he made special alteration on her account, and he assisted her on all occasions in a nice kindly matter of course manner, quite like an elder brother, that prevented any embarrassment on her part. He was also very successful in concealing the anxiety he felt on her behalf. Isabel appeared quite worn out the night they arrived at D—, Norris insisted upon perfect rest and quiet next day, saying that she should join them at tea if she seemed sufficiently rested, but Everard rebelled, and made Emily amuse her during the morning. Norris submitted without much fuss, as he was a great favorite.

"I know as well as you Master Everard, that she needs to be kept more cheerful than she has been, but after all the worry and fatigue of the journey, a little quietness is good for her," said Norris, endeavoring to justify herself.

"I don't deny that Norris, I only object to her being quite alone."

"And you know sir, that you always get your own way," replied Norris laughing.

"Usually," returned Everard, "but Norris, understand that I wish her kept quiet."

"As if anyone could be quiet where Miss Emily is," said Norris reproachfully.

"I'll trust Emmy," he answered laughing.

"That is more nor I would Mr. Everard," she returned with the familiarity that old domestics who have been a long time in a family often acquire. For Norris had been with Mrs. Arlington ever since she was married, now some twenty-six years.

After dinner, Everard, Emily and the children, went out for a ramble. On their return, Everard left them near the town, as he had to make some inquiries as to the time the train left, as he was to leave next morning, for they had been so much longer on the way than had been anticipated, consequently his stay at D—had to be curtailed.

When he returned to the cottage, he found Isabel in the old arm chair in the sitting-room, the others had not yet arrived. Isabel was looking wretchedly ill, but pronounced herself much rested. Everard gave her an animated account of their ramble, and an excellent description of the place, but she appeared to take little interest in either.

"Perhaps you would rather I didn't talk, he said, as she leaned her head wearily upon her hand.

"O, I don't mind," she replied in a tone of such utter indifference that Everard took a book. He did not read however, but sat shading his face with his hand, so as to enable him to contemplate the poor worn face and fragile form of her whom he loved better than life. He pictured her, as she appeared when waiting the arrival of the guests on Grace's birthday, and the contrast was painful in the extreme, neither could he account for the utter hopelessness depicted on her countenance.

"Are you aware that I leave in the morning," he said, after some time had elapsed.

"So soon," she inquired in surprise.

"Yes, by the early train," he replied.

Then I must not miss this opportunity of thanking you, for all the trouble you have taken, and for all the kindness you have shown me. Indeed I am very much obliged to you."

"I am only too glad to have been of any service to you," he

returned with something of the old manner. "Will you not write when you are able, if only a line, just a line, I shall be so anxious to hear."

"Emily will write," she answered quietly.

Everard bit his lip, he was silenced but not satisfied,—an awkward pause ensued, then the others came in full of glee to find Isabel down.

The tea was a very cheerful one, and Isabel strove to appear interested, and to join in the general conversation, but the effort was too much for her, for when she rose to retire for the night, she all but fainted and alarmed them very much.

When Everard came into the sitting-room next morning, he found a cheerful fire burning (for the morning was raw and misty) and breakfast on the table, although it was only half-past five o'clock, and shortly after Emily came in.

"Why Emmy, this is better luck than I expected," exclaimed Everard in surprise.

"You didn't think that I would let you breakfast alone did you," returned Emily proceeding to pour out the tea, "but oh, Everard, I'm so sorry that you are going away so soon, I really am quite afraid to be left alone with Isabel so weak, whatever shall I do if she gets worse."

"As to being alone, why Norris is a host in herself. Besides, you must take it for granted that she will soon get all right. If there really should be cause you must not hesitate to call in the doctor, but remember Dr. Heathfield said you were not to do so, if it could be avoided, and Emmy, if there should be anything serious, mind you telegraph mamma, and if you get very much alarmed, you know that I could get here in a few hours, and I shall not mind the trouble, so make yourself easy. But at all events, I intend to run down in two or three weeks, just to see how you all get on—mind you write often Emmy." This Emmy promised to do, and bid him good bye with a bright face.

D—was a pretty little town on the sea-coast, which was much frequented in summer, but during the winter it was almost deserted. It was very quiet just now as it was so very early in the season. The house in which our party had taken up their abode, was beautifully situated upon some rising ground, about half a mile from the beach. On the right, as far as eye could reach, stretched the broad expanse of deep blue sea, with its ever varying succession of white sails and gay steamers. To the left lay verdant meadows, picturesque villas, and sloping hills, stretching far into the distance until bounded by a belt of forest, beyond which the ground rose again, capped by a rugged crag. Belonging to the house, were pretty grounds tastefully laid out, and a nice shrubbery, also a maze in which the children delighted to lose themselves.

After the first few days, Isabel mended rapidly, and before long was able to join the children and Emily in their rambles, and even got down to the beach after the second week, so that Emily sent charming accounts of Isabel's progress to her mother and Everard.

CHAPTER XI

"Look Louis, what a nice packet has come by express, I wonder what it can be. Oh, open it now dear Louis," she added, laying her hand coaxingly upon his shoulder, as he was about to pocket the wonderful packet. "I am dying with curiosity, to see what it contains."

"It is only a business affair, nothing to interest you, little curiosity," he answered playfully.

But she was not so easily satisfied, for the start of recognition as he glanced at the writing, had not escaped his wife's quick eyes.

"But I do so want to know what is in it, I felt something hard like a little box, and it is such pretty writing," she said.

"Perhaps the drugs I wrote for," he returned carelessly.

"Drugs from a lady, Louis," she said archly.

"Oh I forgot, no it can't be the drugs, but it will keep," he replied, thrusting it into his pocket. "I must teach you not to be so curious Natalie.

Then laughing, she endeavored to withdraw it from his

pocket, but he took the little hand in an iron grasp, saying "don't be silly Natalie."

"Oh Louis, you hurt me," she pouted.

"I didn't intend to do so," he returned, loosening his hold, but there was a stern, determined look in his face as he did so, which prevented her making any further attempts to satisfy her curiosity, and the large tears welled up into her eyes as he hastily left the room.

That night, after Natalie had retired to rest, Louis stood leaning against the chimney-piece, gazing thoughtfully into the fire. Upon the table lay the packet, he knew well enough the moment he saw it what it contained, the letters and presents that Isabel had received from himself. Yes there they were, and he would not for worlds have Natalie see them. There they were, the letters, the trinkets, but he had expected something more—an angry note, upbraiding him for his mean conduct and requesting the return of her letters. Over this he would have rejoiced, but no, here were the letters and trinkets without note or comment, just enclosed in a blank cover, and this cool contempt annoyed him more than the bitterest expressions of angry reproach would have done. She had returned all that he had ever given her, well, what else had he expected, did he think she would have kept them? No, of course not, but then he had not thought about it, he knew now that his revenge had had a very different effect to what he had intended, she would cast off all further regard for him, perhaps she hated him, while he, trusting to her sweet disposition and deep affection for himself, had expected that she, unable to overcome her wondrous love, would pine and grieve over her great, her irreparable loss. Ah Louis, if this was your object you did not manage the affair skilfully. You also forgot that by marrying another, you were taking perhaps, the only step that could effectually prevent the object you had in view, (for this, together with the offensive manner in which it was done, supplied her with a motive which aided essentially to enable her to carry out her determination to stifle all feelings of love towards him, in fact to forget him.) He now saw the folly of the course he had adopted, she would soon forget him altogether, perhaps find another more patient and gentle, who could make her happier than he would have done, such thoughts as these were madness—perhaps she might marry another, no, he clinched his fist and vowed she should not. How had his so called revenge recoiled upon himself, he had not been aware how madly he loved her, until she was lost to him forever, and he almost cursed the filthy lucre that had lured him on until it had been his ruin. For what had he gained—he new what he had lost, the only woman that he had ever loved or could love, but what had he gained, not the satisfaction which he had expected, only a few thousand dollars and a pretty childish little wife of whom he already tired.

With an angry exclamation he threw the whole packet into the fire, and then leaning his face upon his hand, before an open book, sat still and pale through the long long night, until in the gray dawn, a soft little hand upon his shoulder, and a warm kiss upon his cheek, aroused him from his reverie.

CHAPTER XII

There was a large rock, about a mile to the left of the town of D—, which was surrounded by numerous small ones. This place was called the wrecker's reef, and was covered at high water, but when the tide was low, Isabel and the others often went there to get shells. They had to be careful to watch the rise of the tide, as, long before the rock was covered the retreat was cut off by the water surrounding the largest rock, like an island, this island gradually diminished, until, when the tide was in it was several feet under water, this part of the coast was very little frequented. One afternoon when they had been at D—about three weeks or a month, having obtained the shells they wished for, they sat down on the rocks to rest, Isabel began relating a tale she had lately read, and they were all so much interested, that they had not observed that the tide was fast coming in, nor was it until the rock was quite surrounded that they did so. The terrified children clung around Isabel entreating her to save them, while Emily scarcely less alarmed, screamed aloud for help, but it was not very likely that her cries for assistance would be heard in that lonely place, and their danger became more imminent, as a stiff breeze had sprung up, and the surge round the reef was becoming very heavy, and even should they be observed, the passage from the beach to the reef was so dangerous, that only a skilful and experienced hand could possibly succeed in rescuing them from their perilous

Clotilda Jennings

situation, so that although there was a small boat moored on the beach it did not afford them much consolation. They were constantly drenched with spray, and were quite aware that the reef would be covered with water ere long.

"Oh dearest Isabel, what shall we do," asked Emily, looking ghastly white, and shaking like an aspen.

"The water will wash us all away, and then we shall all be drowned," cried little Amy.

"And we shall never see papa and mamma any more,' added Rose. Alice stood perfectly quiet, (after the first moment of their surprise when she had clung to Isabel with the rest) her large eyes fixed upon Isabel with an expression that spoke volumes.

"I fear there is no escape," said Isabel, in as calm a tone as she could command, "we can only commend ourselves to the care of our heavenly Father, and patiently await his will. This they did, and then Isabel endeavored to calm litttle Amy, who was crying most piteously, but a shout of joy from Rose, drew her attention once more to the shore. "Here is Everard, oh here is Everard," cried Rose, clapping her hands and dancing with joy, and sure enough, there was Everard scrambling down the cliff. This was Saturday afternoon, and he had come to spend Sunday with them, but finding they were out he came in search of them, Norris, fortunately being able to tell him where they had gone.

As the reef was such a short distance from land, and as a boat was moored on the beach, the children naturally concluded that they were now safe. It was not so however with Isabel, she knew the dangerous nature of this shallow water, with innumerable rocks only just beneath the surface, but still sufficiently covered to hide them from view, which made it very difficult to take a boat safely through them, even when the water was smooth, but how much more so, now that a rough swell was foaming over them. Indeed it was only by taking a zig-zag course, that any boat could be guided in safety through the labyrinth of rocks. As Everard was quite unacquainted with the perilous nature of the reef, it was well that Isabel had taken particular notice of the only passage and its curious windings, so that they were enabled to direct him how to steer, or the boat would assuredly have been knocked to pieces, and they all would inevitably have perished. But fortunately Everard was the crack oar of the college club, and the owner of the champion medal, and in spite of all difficulties managed to make his way to the reef.

Isabel had watched the progress of the boat with intense anxiety, her heart beat fast, for she expected every moment that it would come to grief, and she experienced an indescribable sensation of apprehension when it grated on the rock on which they stood.

"Oh, this boat won't hold us all," exclaimed Emily in dismay.

"Don't leave me," entreated little Amy, "please don't."

"No darling, you shall not be left," said Isabel kissing her and then lifting her into the boat. Quickly as this was done, Rose was already in; Isabel insisted upon both Emily and Alice going, though the boat was by this means very heavily laden—Alice would have remained with her, but Isabel would not allow it, as there was every prospect of the reef being entirely covered before the boat could possibly return.

"But it seems so mean to leave you here alone." urged Alice.

"It will not mend matters, if two are washed off instead of one," whispered Isabel, "go dear Alice while you can."

"But it seems so mean," she repeated.

"Come Alice," said Everard in a tone that settled the question at once, "every minute is of the greatest importance." It was agony to him to leave Isabel, but there was no help for it, the boat was now loaded down to the water's edge. He would gladly have let Alice remain, had there appeared any chance of returning in time, for he would have gained several minutes by so doing, for if the boat had been lighter he could have made better time. As it was he did not dare to risk it, for it seemed like dooming Alice to destruction needlessly. But oh, the horror of leaving Isabel when perhaps she would be washed away by the fast rising tide before he could return. This thought had also decided him to take Alice, for should Isabel be washed off he might be able to save her, but how could he hope to save two in such untoward circumstances.

"Courage Miss Leicester," and the boat seemed to fly through the water with each vigorous stroke; his face wore an expression of intense anxiety as he bent to his oars. No words passed his firmly compressed lips after they left the reef, but his contracted brow and heavy breathing revealed how deeply he was suffering. In an incredibly short time they reached the beach, and Everard landed them in a very unceremonies manner, and then started once more for the rock. Notwithstanding all the exertion he had undergone, his face was as pale as death, and the cold damp stood upon his brow. There was an air of determination about him as he sprang back into the boat, that convinced Emily that he would save Isabel or perish in the attempt, and from that day she was master of his secret, but like a dear good sister as she was, she kept it in her kind little heart, though she sometimes built castles in the air.

Knowing now the proper course to take, Everard propelled the boat with marvellous rapidity, it skimmed over the water like an ocean bird, at least so Rose said; yet when he reached the reef, every part on which it was possible to stand was covered with water, and it was with the greatest difficulty that Isabel contrived to cling to a pointed piece of rock which still remained above water, nor could she have done so much longer, as her strength was fast failing. It seemed to Isabel wondrous strange, that she should feel so anxious to be rescued from her perilous situation, when not so long ago she had been so desirous of death, but so it was.

It was no easy matter to get the boat to this point, and had it required any more water to float it, it would have been impossible. As soon as Isabel was in the boat a joyful shout was raised by the party on shore. The return to land was slow, as the great exertion he had been forced to use was beginning to tell upon Everard. Of course Isabel was soaking wet, but fortunately a large plaid that Norris had made them take with them had been left on the beach; this they wrapt round her, and then went home as quickly as might be.

"Mercy on us," exclaimed Norris, as they made their appearance, "what in the name of wonder have you been doing."

"Why getting a soaking don't you see," returned Isabel, much amused at Norris's manner.

"Then you will just get to bed right away Miss Leicester, for I would like to know how I am to answer to my Misses and Dr. Heathfield, if you get the consumption through your nonsense, dear me, and you were looking so well."

"But Norris, if I change these wet things surely that will do."

"You just get to bed, I say, for you are in my charge."

Everard laughed.

"Now Mr. Everard don't you be a interfering."

"Oh, certainly not."

"Now come along at once Miss Leicester, and I will get you some hot gruel." Isabel did as she was bid, not wishing to vex Norris who had been very kind, but she protested against the gruel, but in vain, Norris made her swallow a large basin full, which to Isabel's intense disgust had a plentiful supply of brandy in it. After this Norris consented to hear the history of their adventures, which was told by the whole five at once.

"The air of D—seems to have done wonders," said Everard when Isabel made her appearance at breakfast next morning looking quite her former self.

"Yes indeed," returned Isabel with a pleasant smile, "how very stupid you must have thought us yesterday, I can't imagine how we could have been so foolish."

"I suppose that you were not aware that the reef would be covered as the tide rose."

"Oh yes, we knew quite well."

"Well then, you were all awfully stupid, if you will excuse my saying so," returned Everard, "I gave you credit Miss Leicester for more prudence."

"You may well be surprised," Isabel answered coloring, "I am afraid when Mrs. Arlington hears of it she will be of Lady Ashton's opinion, that I am not fit to have charge of her daughters."

Emily laughed.

"Did she say that," said Everard, "it was very impertinent of her."

"She thinks herself a privileged person, you would be astonished I can tell you if you heard all that she said."

"Do be quiet Emily," interrupted Isabel.

But Emily kept giving provoking little hints all breakfast time, and even as they walked to church she let out little bits, until Isabel grew almost angry. Everard admired the church exceedingly, "that is just such a church as I would like," he said as they went home.

"Oh Everard," exclaimed Emily, "a little bit of a church like that."

"It is not so small," he returned.

"Oh well, I thought you were more ambitious, if I were a clergyman I should wish to preach to a crowded assembly in a very large city church, and make a sensation."

"Emily!"

"Oh don't look so grave."

"A man that would care about making a sensation, would not be fit to be a clergyman."

"Oh Everard, I am sure it is only good clergymen that do make a sensation."

"What do you call making a sensation?" he inquired.

"Why, to have every body saying what a splendid preacher, and praising you up to the skies."

"Of course every clergyman should aim to be a good preacher, but his sermon should be composed with the object of doing as much good as possible, the idea of getting praise by it should never enter his head."

"Of course I know I never should have done for a parson, if I had been a man I should have been a—."

"Lawyer," the children all shouted in a breath.

"Or a midshipman," said Emily.

"I wonder what Miss Leicester would have been," observed Rose.

"A doctor," said Emily, "I know she would have been a doctor, wouldn't you Isabel."

Isabel became scarlet, this was only a random suggestion, but it seemed so like the answer the children had given Emily, that it made her color painfully.

"Oh what is the use of talking such nonsense," she replied, but her vivid color had given Emily a new idea; Isabel she whispered "do those pet letters come from a doctor," a shade passed over Isabel's face like a cloud over the sun, as the thought occured that she should get no more pet letters, as Emily chose to call them, for though she had so firmly resolved not to allow her thoughts to dwell upon the past, there were still times when she was painfully reminded of the happy days that would never return, not that she grieved for the loss of Louis, as he now stood revealed in his true character. She knew that it had been her own ideal Louis that she had loved, she had clothed him with virtue that he did not possess, and ascribed to him a nobleness of nature to which he was a stranger, and her bitter sorrow was that he should have proved so different to what she had believed him. She had already begun to think that, as he was what he was, it was all for the best, and even now she felt more of contempt than love regarding him, though nothing short of the offensive and aggravated circumstances that had taken place, could have served to quench such love as her's.

Isabel avoided giving an answer to Emily's question, by drawing attention to a beautiful yacht that was now making the harbor, this did for the time, but Emily had made enough by her venture to plague Isabel sufficiently about the doctor, so much so, that Everard took occasion when they two were walking in the shrubbery to remonstrate with his sister, "Emily," he said, "can't you see that Miss Leicester is really annoyed at your nonsense, and I think that it amounts to rudeness in such a case."

"Oh she don't care about it."

"You are mistaken Emily."

"Oh, but it is such fun, I do so like to make her color up, she looks so pretty."

"But when you see that it really annoys——."

"When I get into the spirit of the thing, I can't stop." interrupted Emily.

"I know it," replied Everard gently, "and that is the reason that I mention it, otherwise the matter is too trivial to comment upon."

The tears stood in Emily's eyes, "I did not mean any harm," she said softly, for Everard had great influence, and the secret of this influence which he had acquired over all the family was, that he was gentle yet very firm.

"I did not say that there was any harm, only you should learn to stop when you see that it annoys, and surely you might abstain from such nonsense on a Sunday, it is setting the children a bad example to say the least of it."

CHAPTER XIII

Isabel and the children remained the greater part of the summer at D—, but Emily returned home to join her mamma and sister, who had consented to join an expedition that had been got up among a few select friends. Upon the last afternoon of their stay at D—they went for a ramble into a pretty little copse wood, the children were looking for berries, and Isabel sat upon a mossy bank reading.

"Come Isabel, let us at least be friends," said a voice close beside her.

Surprised and startled, Isabel beheld Louis Taschereau.

"Let us be friends," he repeated taking a seat on the bank.

"Impossible, Dr. Taschereau," said Isabel rising, "had you broken off your engagement in a straightforward manner, it might have been different, as your feelings had undergone a change, I should have been quite content to release you, but to have corresponded with me up to the very day of your marriage, and allow me by a chance meeting at an evening party to become aware of the fact for the first time, together with the effrontery with which you behaved on that occasion, are insults which I should be wanting in self respect not to resent."

"My feelings have undergone no change, they cannot change, it is you alone that I have ever loved or shall love, my wife I never did, never can. Oh pity me Isabel for I am most miserably unhappy."

"From my heart I pity her who is so unfortunate as to have Dr. Taschereau for a husband," she replied, "I cannot pity you, for if anything could make your conduct more contemptible, it is the fact that you have just acknowledged, that you do not love the girl that you have made your wife, though having seen the way in which you treat those you profess to love it is no great loss, and your happiness must ever be a matter of indifference to me."

"Oh cruel girl, I am not so heartless, what grieves me more than even my own misery is the thought of your suffering."

"Then pray do not distress yourself on my account Dr. Taschereau, whatever I may have felt it is past, for when Isabel Leicester could no longer esteem, she must cease to love."

"I will not believe that you find it so easy to forget me, for that you did love me you dare not deny, it was no passing fancy, you must feel more than you are willing to own," he said angrily.

"I do not wish to deny it," returned Isabel firmly, "but you out to have known me better than to think that I should continue to do so. After you were married it became my duty to forget that I had ever loved you, and to banish every thought of you. You have made your choice and now regrets are useless, even wrong, whatever she may be, she is your wife, and it is your duty and should be your pleasure to make her happy, and as you value happiness, never give her cause to doubt your love."

"As you say, regrets are useless, but that thought only adds to my torture, I can only compare my present wretchedness with the happy lot which might have been mine, but for my own folly," he said sadly, "but you must help me."

"How can I help you," exclaimed Isabel.

"It is you alone who can, for you are the only person who ever had any influence over me, you must help to keep me right. Will you not forgive me Isabel, and let me be a friend—a brother."

"Thank heaven I have no such brother," exclaimed Isabel fervently, "for I should feel very much inclined to disown him if I had. Friends we can never be Dr. Taschereau, as I told you before, whenever and wherever we meet, it must be as strangers."

"As you will," he said bitterly, "but since you will not have me for your friend, you shall have me for a foe."

"Think not to intimidate me with idle threats," she answered haughtily, "you have no power to harm me, and I feel assured that as your love is worthless, so in the end your hatred will prove harmless."

"That is as it may be, but still I had much rather that we were friends."

"If an enemy, I defy you, my friend you can never be."

"As you will," he returned fiercely, "but remember if I go to the bad, with you will rest the blame," and then he disappeared through the wood.

"And what is his wife about during this conversation, writing to her cousin. Let us take a peep at the letter.

DEAREST MARIE.—I am happy—very happy, how could I be otherwise with my noble Louis, he is so kind, so thoughtful and considerate, he would not let me accompany him to-day, because I was so tired with the journey yesterday, so I take the opportunity thus afforded me to write to you. Oh Marie, how could you ever suppose that he married me for my money, how could you form so mean an opinion of my generous, noble, high minded Louis, you wrong him Marie, indeed you do. True, he is more reserved than is pleasant, but I presume that is because I am so childish as papa used to say. Would you believe I had a jealous fit about a packet that he received from a lady, which he refused to open when I asked him. Well he sat up very very late that night, and I took it into my stupid little head that his sitting up had something to do with the packet, and the thought so possessed me, that I got up and went softly into the library, and there he was in a brown study over some medical work. Oh Marie I felt so ashamed of my foolish fancies.

CHAPTER XIV

Upon the morning after their return to Elm Grove, Isabel requested a few moments conversation with Mrs. Arlington. Desiring Isabel to follow, Mrs. Arlington led the way into the morning-room, and after expressing her great satisfaction at the beneficial results of the sea air, she said "that she hoped Miss Leicester's health was sufficiently restored to enable the children to resume their studies upon the following Monday." Isabel replied "that she was quite well, and was as anxious as Mrs. Arlington could be, that they should lose no more time." Indeed for some weeks past she had been teaching during the morning, but it was not of them that I was about to speak," she continued, "it was of myself, and I trust that you will not blame me for not doing so before I went away, as indeed it was impossible. Dr. Heathelfid was right in thinking that my illness was caused by mental suffering, it was indeed a severe shock," she added, covering her face with her hands, for it was a trial to Isabel, and it cost her a great deal this self imposed task.

"Defer this communication if it distresses you," said Mrs. Arlington kindly.

"Oh no, I would rather tell you," but it was not without some difficulty that Isabel continued, "sometime before my father's death, I was though, unknown to him, engaged to a medical student, I always regretted concealing our engagement from him in the first instance. I knew it was very wrong, but Louis made me promise not to tell my father, or breathe a word about our engagement to any living soul. I asked him why, but he would give no reason except that he wished it. I promised, but had I known that it was for more than a short period, I think that I should not have done so. About six months afterwards, when his uncle was about to send him to France to a relation who was a celebrated physician, he wanted me to be married privately, this I positively refused, I said that whilst my father lived I would never marry without his consent, and urged him to let me acquaint my father of our engagement. This he refused, I told him that I was sure my father would not object, but he would not listen to me, it was absurd he said, to suppose that he would let us marry if he knew of it, for he was entirely dependent upon his uncle, and had positively nothing of his own as yet, but hoped soon to rise in his profession; if we were once married he argued, my father would storm a little at first, but would soon give in, and make some arrangement that would prevent his going away, in vain I entreated to be allowed to plead our cause with my father. Louis was inexorable upon that point, he dare not he said, and used every argument to induce me to accede to his wishes and agree to his propositions; but when I resisted all entreaties he was mortally offended, and got into a terrible passion, it seems he never forgave me for thwarting him, but I was not aware of it, for after his anger had cooled down our parting was most kind. During my father's illness, my secret became an intolerable burden, oh, how bitterly I suffered for deceiving so indulgent a parent, and yet my conscience would not allow me to break my promise. I wrote to Louis imploring him to give the desired permission, and received a very kind letter, assuring me that my altered circumstances would make no difference to him, that in fact the only barrier between us was now removed, but the longed for permission was withheld, Louis did not notice that part of my letter in anyway. Shortly after this, my poor father died—died without ever having heard of our engagement, his greatest pain in parting from his darling child, being the grief he felt at leaving her so unprotected, Imagine if you can my grief and misery," said Isabel shedding bitter tears of agony and remorse at the remembrance of that dreadful time, and what it must have been to witness his anguish, as over and over again he would say "oh my child, could I but have left you to the tender care of a beloved husband, or even could I know that you were the promised wife of one who truly loved you, I could die in peace, even though he were not rich in this world's goods, but to leave you thus my darling child, to make your own way in this wicked world is almost more than I can bear." "What good" continued Isabel "could I expect after such a return for all dear papa's fond indulgence and unvaried kindness. After my father's death, I received a letter from Louis full of love and sympathy, and approving of my plans, as it would be some time before he would be in a position to marry. We continued to correspond until the night of the ball, at which Dr. and Mrs. Taschereau were among the guests, then I learned for the first time that he was faithless and unworthy. You do not know what I suffered, nor his cruel triumph, or you would not wonder that it should end as it did. I have told you all this Mrs. Arlington because I thought it my duty, and also, that should Dr. Taschereau again be your guest, you might kindly spare me the pain of meeting him."

"Poor child you have suffered greatly," said Mrs. Arlington kindly. She had listened very patiently and very attentively to all Isabel had to say, but she had not said how that she already knew something of this from her own delirious talk during her illness, but she thought that it would make Isabel uncomfortable, therefore she remained silent upon that point. "You may depend that I shall not abuse your confidence" she

Clotilda Jennings

continued, "I do not promise secrecy, but you may trust to my discretion without fear. Whenever you need advice, do not scruple to come to me, as I shall always be glad to give it," no doubt, but Isabel was the last person to ask advice, though she had the highest opinion of Mrs. Arlington.

"I think you would do well Isabel, to re-consider the offer I made you to visit with my daughters."

"You are very kind; but, indeed, I would rather not."

"As you please, Miss Leicester; but I think you are wrong to refuse. You may be sure that the offer is disinterested on my part." (Disinterested it certainly was, as neither of the Arlington girls could compare favorably with Isabel as to beauty or accomplishments.)

"I fully appreciate your kindness, Mrs. Arlington, but indeed it would be extremely unpleasant to do so," returned Isabel.

"I cannot let this opportunity pass without expressing my gratitude for your great kindness during my illness, for I can never, never repay you. But I will use my best endeavors to make your children all that you can wish."

"And that will quite repay me," replied Mrs. Arlington, kindly.

CHAPTER XV

Upon a beautiful moonlight night, under the trees in the garden of Madame Bourges' boarding-school, near Versailles, quite secure from observation stood Arthur Barrington and Louisa Aubray, engaged in earnest conversation.

"Are you happy here, dearest Louisa?" he inquired, in accents of deepest tenderness.

"Happy! Ah, no, Louisa is never happy," she answered, "but lonely and unhappy—so unhappy and miserable!"

"But you are not lonely now that I am here, dear Louisa."

"No; but, when you are gone, it is so dreary—oh, so dreary!"

"You used to think that you would be so happy at school."

"Ah, yes! but I'm not. Madame is harsh, the teachers cruel, and the girls so strange: they do not love me," she cried, in a burst of passionate weeping; "nobody loves Louisa!"

"Oh, Louisa, dearest Louisa, do not say so!" he exclaimed passionately; "do not say that nobody loves you, when I have come so far expressly to see if you are happy. I love you,

Louisa, with all the warmth of my ardent nature, with undying affection. I want you to be mine—MINE! that I may guard you from every ill but such as I can share."

"Oh! can you—will you—do this, Arthur? Will you, indeed, share all my troubles and sorrows, nor deem them, when the first full joy of love is past, unworthy of your attention—your cares, too great to admit of such trifles, claiming your consideration? If you will, and also let me share all your joys and griefs in perfect sympathy and love, then—then my dream of happiness will be fulfilled; but if, in years to come," she continued, with suppressed emotion, "you should change, and a harshness or indifference take the place of sympathy and love, Oh I would wish to die before that day!"

"Dearest Louisa, can you doubt me?"

"I will trust you, Arthur, but I have seen that which makes me almost doubt the existence of love and happiness. I can picture to myself the home of love and peace that I would have. Is it an impossibility; is it but an ideal dream?"

"May it be a blessed reality, my darling Louisa!" he exclaimed, with ardor, as he clasped her passionately in his arms. She made no resistance, but, with her head resting upon his breast, she said, in a tone of deep earnestness:

"If you loved me always, and were always kind, oh Arthur, I I could do anything—suffer anything—for your sake, and care for naught beyond our home. But, my nature is not one" she continued impetuously, "that can be slighted, crushed, and treated with unkindness or indifference, and endure it patiently. No!" she added, with suppressed passion, "a fierce flame of resentment, bitterness, perchance even hatred, would spring up and sweep all kindly feelings far away!"

"Oh, Louisa, Louisa!" interrupted Arthur in a tone of tender remonstrance, "why do you speak in this dreadful manner— why do you doubt my love and constancy?"

The impetuous mood was gone, and a trusting confidence succeeded it. She fixed her eyes upon his face with an expression of unutterable tenderness, as she answered, in a sweet, soft voice, "I love you, Arthur; I cannot doubt you; you are all the world to me."

"Then you will leave here as soon as I can make arrangements for our marriage."

"How gladly, how joyfully, I cannot tell!" she replied, smiling sweetly through her tears. "Tell me again that you love me; I do so want some one to love me! Is it true that you do, indeed, or is it only a beautiful dream? I have lived so desolate and alone that I can scarcely believe my happiness."

"You may believe it, Louisa, it is no dream; my love for you is no passing fancy—it is true and sincere, and will last till life shall end," he said, kissing her tenderly.

"Ha, ha!" laughed Lucy Mornington, as she came full upon the lovers, "Now I have found you out, Miss Aubray; I wondered what was up. Oh, if Madame could only see you, what a scene there would be!" she cried, dancing about and laughing immoderately."

"How dare you come here?" exclaimed Louisa, her large eyes flashing angrily, while her whole frame trembled with passion. "How dare you follow and watch me, how dare you?" she repeated.

"Hush, Louisa!" said Arthur, soothingly, "Lucy is never ill-natured. You have nothing to fear, for I am sure she would not be unkind; and we must not mind her laughing, as I'm afraid that either of us would have done the same if placed in the same unexpected position."

Louisa now clung to Lucy, weeping violently, and imploring her in the most winning manner not to betray them to Madame.

"Don't be afraid, Louisa; Lucy and I were always good friends, and, now I come to think of it, she will be a most valuable assistant. I am sure we may trust her," and he looked inquiringly at Lucy.

"That, you may," answered Lucy; "but there is no earthly use in trying to keep a secret from me, as that is utterly impossible; but whatever you may have to say, you must defer to a more auspicious moment, for Mademoiselle Mondelet has missed Louisa, and she is hunting everywhere for her. So make yourself scarce, Mr. Arthur; we will enter the chapel by a secret door that I discovered in some of my marauding expeditions, and they will never imagine that we came from the garden. Come along, Louisa."

"Adieu! Lucy, and many thanks for your warning, for I certainly don't want Mademoiselle to find me here. Farewell, dearest Louisa; I will be here at this time to-morrow evening," said Arthur, and then he quickly disappeared.

Lucy and Louisa went into the chapel, and the former commenced playing the organ, which she often did. So that when Mademoiselle came into the chapel, by-and-bye, fuming about Louisa, Lucy replied, with the greatest coolness, "Oh, we have been here ever so long."

Shortly after this, Isabel received the following epistle from Lucy:

DEAREST ISABEL,—I am at school again, instead of being in London enjoying myself as I expected. I am cooped up in this abominable place. I suppose Mamma thinks me too wild. Heigho! But, never mind; Ada and Charles are going to remain three years in London, so you see I still have a chance. Ah, me! I think I should die of *ennui* in this dismal place (which was once an abbey, or a convent, or something of the sort, I believe,) but, fortunately for me, an event has occurred which has just put new life in my drooping spirits. We have // who in the name of wonder do you think the parties were? Arthur Barrington and Louisa Aubray. Oh, what a rage Lady Ashton will be in! Don't be shocked, my pet, when I tell you that I went into the affair with all my heart and soul, and was bridesmaid at the interesting ceremony. Oh, Isabel, Arthur is so thoroughly nice that I almost envied Louisa her husband. We managed everything so beautifully that they were married and off upon their travels before Madame found out that there was anything in the wind. And the best of the fun was that Arthur brought a clergyman friend with him, and they were married in the school chapel at four o'clock in the morning. Of course this sweet little piece of fun is not known, and is never likely to be. I enjoyed the whole thing immensely. Of course they don't know that I had anything to do with the affair. Woe betide me if they did! If Louisa had had a father and mother, I would not have had anything to do with it; but, under present circumstances, I thought it was the best thing she could do. So I helped them all I could—in fact I contrived it all for them—when I once found out what they were up to.

Yours, at present, in the most exuberant spirits,
LUCY MORNINGTON.

P.S.—The happy pair have gone to Switzerland or Italy.

Clotilda Jennings

"Here, Emily," said Isabel, when Emily came in, "I think this will amuse you."

"I think Arthur and Louisa did very wrong," she resumed, when Emily had finished reading.

"Ah, well, I have not much fancy for secret marriages, but in this case it was unavoidable, if they were to marry at all," said Emily, laughing.

"But I thought that second cousins couldn't marry."

"They can't, I believe; but then Arthur and Louisa are no relation—for though he always calls Lady Ashton 'Aunt,' she is not his aunt in reality. Don't you know Lord Barrington's first wife was Lady Ashton's sister, and Arthur's mother was the second wife; so you see they are no relations," replied Emily. "Oh, what a rage Lady Ashton will be in!" she resumed. Don't you know that Louisa's father was Arthur's tutor. There was a dreadful quarrel between the two families about that marriage; they wouldn't speak for years, and the old folks are barely civil to each other when they meet even now. But she likes Arthur. What a good thing it is that she is going to stay away so long. But I'm sorry about Lucy; we shall miss her at Christmas."

"So we shall, but May and Peter will be here, and they are a host in themselves."

"But May can't be compared to Lucy; I will have her come; I will tell Harry so. She can come out with her papa and mamma, and go back in the spring. And now, my dear, guess what I came to tell you."

"Rose told me your brother was to come to-day."

"What a sieve Rose is," exclaimed Emily. "But I have more than that to tell. I have a letter from Harry; he is coming soon, and has passed his examination already. What do you think of that?" and she looked so triumphant and delighted.

"Why, Emily, how ever could you read my letter, and discuss the news it contained, when you came on purpose to tell me? I declare, wonders never will cease."

"The fact is that I was so astonished to hear about the elopement, that I almost forgot about my own letter for the time."

"I suppose Harry will make a long stay now? that will be very nice."

"No, he says he can only stay a week, or perhaps a fortnight. He has promised a friend to go to the Blue Mountains," pouted Emily; "I wish his friend was at Jericho."

Isabel laughed. "Suppose in that case Harry had gone with him."

"Don't be provoking, Isabel. But, to turn the table, how is it you never get any of those 'nice letters' now-a-days."

"Don't be provoking, Emily!" said Isabel, growing very hot.

"Ah, you see I always get the best of it," returned Emily, laughing. "I must go and dress, for I have to make some calls with Mamma and Grace."

CHAPTER XVI

"I do not know what on earth they will do," cried Emily, tossing her hat and gloves on the sofa. "Everard is in a terrible stew about the anthem; Mary Cleaver is laid up with a bad cold and sore throat, so that there is no chance of her being able to sing to-morrow, and there is not another in the choir that could make anything of the solo—at least not anything worth listening to. Is it not provoking?—just at the last minute. Grace, now won't you take Miss Cleaver's place just for once? Do, please."

"Thanks! But the idea is too absurd. Fancy my singing at a 'missionary meeting.'"

"Perhaps Isabel would," interposed Rose.

"The idea is too absurd," returned Emily, affectedly.

"Don't be impertinent, Emily," said Grace, haughtily. "It is useless to talk of Isabel, she added, addressing Rose, "she refused before, and Everard would not be so absurd as to ask her again; he was quite pressing enough—far too much so for my taste."

"I'm not so sure he won't; he will not easily give up his 'pet anthem,'" replied Emily.

"Well, Isabel will not do it, you will see," answered Grace.

"I'm not so sure of that, either; he usually gets his own way somehow or other."

"Then how was it he did not succeed at first?" said Grace, tartly.

"Oh, because Isabel made him believe that it would not be fair to Miss Cleaver."

"Oh, Emily, that was not why Isabel would not, and she never said it was," exclaimed Alice; "she told Everard she had several reasons for not singing, and, she added, it would not be fair to Miss Cleaver after being in the choir so long."

"And pray what might these weighty reasons be?" asked Grace.

"I don't know," returned Alice.

"Nor Isabel, either, I imagine," Grace answered.

"What are you so perturbed about, Emily?" asked Isabel, who now joined them."

"The choir are in trouble about the anthem."

"How is that?" inquired Isabel.

"Mary Cleaver is sick," returned Emily, "and Everard is awfully put out about it."

Everard entered with a roll of music in his hand.

"Where is Miss Leicester?" he asked.

"She is here," Grace answered, languidly.

"You will not now refuse to take the soprano in the anthem to-morrow, he said, when I tell you that it is utterly impossible for Miss Cleaver to do so, and that the anthem must be omitted unless you will sing."

"I am sorry that the anthem should be a failure, but I really cannot," replied Isabel, evidently annoyed.

"Oh, yes you can—just this once," he pleaded.

But Isabel only shook her head.

"Do you mean, Miss Leicester, that you positively will not?" he asked.

"Seriously, Mr. Arlington, I do not intend to sing in the choir to-morrow."

"That is your final decision?"

"Yes."

He sat beating his foot impatiently on the ground.

"Is there no one else? Everard" asked Rose.

"No one!" he answered, in a very decided tone.

He tossed the music idly in his hand, though his brow contracted, and the veins in his forehead swelled like cords. They were very quiet; no one spoke. Emily enjoyed this little scene immensely, but Grace was highly disgusted that her brother should deign to urge a request which had already been denied, and that, too, by the governess; while Isabel sat, thinking how very kind Everard had always been, and how ill-natured it seemed to refuse—how much she wished to oblige—but the thing was so distasteful that she felt very averse to comply. She remembered, too, the beautiful flowers with which Alice had kept her vases constantly supplied when she was recovering from her illness; she knew full well to whom she was indebted for them, as but one person in the house dare cull the choicest flowers with such a lavish hand.

"What are you waiting for, Everard?" Emily inquired, at length.

"For Isabel to relent," said Grace, contemptuously.

Everard rose, and stood for a moment irresolute; then, going to the piano, set up the music, and, turning to Isabel, said in a tone of deep earnestness: "Will you oblige me by just trying this, Miss Leicester?"

Grace's lip curled scornfully, and Isabel reluctantly seated herself at the piano. Having once commenced, she thought of nothing but the beauty of the anthem, and sung with her whole soul—her full, rich voice filling the room with melody. Never had Isabel sung like this since she had left her happy home. When she ceased they all crowded round her, entreating her to take Miss Cleaver's place just this once.

"She will—she must!" exclaimed Everard, eagerly. "You will—will you not, Isa—Miss Leicester?" he asked persuasively.

Isabel was silent.

"A nice example of obliging manners you are setting your pupils," said Emily, mischievously, at the same time hugging her affectionately. "What makes my pet so naughty to-day?"

"I suppose I must," said Isabel, in a tone of annoyance; "I see that I shall have no peace if I don't."

"Thanks, Miss Leicester," said Everard, warmly; "I can't tell you how much—how very much—obliged I am."

"I should not imagine that such a very ungracious compliance called for such excessive thanks," said Grace, sarcastically.

"Don't be ill-natured, Gracie," returned her brother, laughing; "you don't know how glad I am."

"But it is so very absurd, Everard, the way you rave about Isabel's singing, any one would suppose that you had never heard good singing."

"Nor have I, before, ever heard such singing as Miss Leicester's," he returned.

"Oh, indeed, how very complimentary we are to-day!" retorted Grace.

"Such singing as Miss Leicester's!" echoed Isabel, with a gesture of contempt which set Emily laughing excessively, while Everard beat a hasty retreat.

In the evening Emily and Isabel had their things on, and were chatting and laughing with the children in the school-room, before going down to the church for the practising, when Mrs. Arlington came in, saying, "I am afraid that you will all be disappointed, but Dr. Heathfield strictly prohibits Miss Leicester taking any part in the singing to-morrow."

"Oh, Mamma!" exclaimed Emily.

"He says that it would be highly dangerous, and that she must not attempt it."

"But, Mamma, we cannot have the anthem without her."

"I am very sorry, my dear, but it cannot be helped," replied her mother, and having given them the unpleasant tidings to digest as best they might, Mrs. Arlington returned to the drawing-room.

"Now is not that too bad? Who in the world told Dr. Heathfield anything about it, I should like to know?" cried Emily, indignantly. "What possessed him to come here to-night, I wonder—tiresome old fellow?"

"But if it would really do Isabel harm, I think it was very fortunate he came," said Alice, gravely.

"Oh be quiet, Alice! you only provoke me," returned Emily.

"Are you young ladies ready?" asked Everard.

"Oh, Miss Leicester is not going to sing," cried Rose, saucily. "What will you do now?"

"What do you mean?" he asked, looking inquiringly from one to another.

"Why," said Emily, "Dr. Heathfield has forbidden anything of the kind, and was quite peppery about it."

"Confound Dr. Heathfield!" he exclaimed angrily. "Is this true?" he asked, turning to Isabel.

"Yes."

"It is all nonsense! I shall speak to Heathfield about it."

"That will do no good, Everard," interposed Emily; "He told mamma that Isabel ought not to think of doing so at present."

"You did not think it would hurt you Miss Leicester," he asked.

"Never for a moment."

"I dare say he thinks you are going to join the choir altogether, I shall tell him that it is only the anthem to-morrow, that you intend taking part in, surely he cannot object to that." What passed between them did not transpire, but when Everard returned he said to Isabel in a tone of deep earnestness, "I should not have asked you to sing, had I known the harm it might possibly do you, indeed I would not, and though annoyed beyond measure at having to give up the anthem, I am very glad that Dr. Heathfield's opportune visit prevented you running such a risk, for had any serious consequences ensued, I alone should have been to blame."

"No one would have been to blame, all being unaware of any danger," returned Isabel warmly, "but I am convinced that Dr. Heathfield is considering possibilities, though not probabilities" she added coloring, not well satisfied to be thought so badly of."

"Tell us what he said, Everard," petitioned Emily.

"He spoke very strongly and warned me not to urge her," Everard replied evidently unwilling to say more.

"I don't believe that it could harm me," said Isabel thought-fully, "but of course—."

"You are jolly glad to get off," chimed in Rose saucily, and received a reproof from Everard.

"We cannot disregard what he says," continued Isabel finishing the sentence.

"Certainly not," returned Everard, and so the anthem was omitted.

CHAPTER XVII

Alone in tears sits Natalie, alas she has awakened from her dream of bliss, to the sad reality that she is an unloved neglected wife, and bitter very bitter is this dreadful truth to the poor little bird far far from all who love her, for the wide ocean rolls between them, poor little humming bird formed for sunshine and happiness, how cans't thou bear this sad awakening. Ah cherished little one, with what bright hopes of love and happiness dids't thou leave a sunny home, and are they gone for ever, oh what depth of love in thy crushed and bleeding heart, striving ever to hide beneath a sunny face thy aching heart, lest it should grieve or vex the husband thou lovest so fondly, while he heedlessly repelling the loving one whose happiness depends upon his kindness, or impatiently receiving the fond caress, discerns not the breaking heart nor the secret anguish this same indifference causes; Ah Louis, Louis, should not one so bright and gentle, receive something better than impatient gestures and harsh words, which send the stream of love back with a thrilling pain to the heart, to consume it with silent agony, and her hope has proved vain, her babe, her darling babe has not accomplished what she fondly imagined, brought back her Louis's love, if indeed she ever possessed it, and it is this thought which wrings her gentle heart and causes those sobs of anguish, that make her fragile form to quiver like an aspen, as the storm of grief will have its course. If indeed he ever loved her, that he does not now is clear enough; but did he ever, why should she doubt it, she has accidentally heard the following remarks, and seen Louis pointed out as the object of them:

He was engaged to a beautiful girl, but she was poor, so meeting with an heiress, he was dazzled by the prospect of wealth and married her; but the marriage had proved an unhappy one, that Mr. T—had soon tired of his gay little wife, and now treated her with the greatest indifference and neglect, and that having married her solely for her money, he was as much as ever attached to Miss—and bitterly repented his folly. It may be true she sighed, for she knew in her heart that the part regarding his treatment of herself was but alas too true; but could he indeed love another, no, she would not believe it, she would dismiss the thought, but still the words rung in her ears, having married her solely for her money. Could Marie be right, but no, no, she would not, could not believe it, O Louis, Louis, how have I loved you, how I love you still, and is my love entirely unrequited? And now a new feeling springs up in her heart, bitter hatred towards her unknown rival, with beating heart and trembling lips she calls to mind the packet and Louis's embarrassment, the beautiful miniature she had seen by accident, and his evasive answers when questioned about the original, could she be the Isabel he had named her darling after, in spite of all she could urge as to her great dislike of the name. Oh that she could confide all her troubles to him and tell him all her fears, and if possible have her mind set at rest, but she dare not, for though she loved him so devotedly, she feared him too, his fierce bursts of passion frightened her. Oh I will win his love in spite of this hateful girl, I will be so gentle, so careful to please him, so mindful of his comfort (as if poor thing she had not always been so) that he shall forget her, and love his own little wife, and wearied with conflicting emotions, she laid her head upon the table and sobbed herself

Clotilda Jennings

to sleep, and thus Louis found her at two o'clock in the morning, when he returned from attending a patient. "Good gracious! Natalie, what are you doing here," said he raising her from her uncomfortable position, "why you are quite chilled," he continued as a convulsive shudder shook her whole frame, "what ever possessed you to sit up, and the fire out, how could you be so foolish." She raised her large dark eyes to his with an expression intensely sad and entreating, and whispered "O Louis, tell me do you love me!" he could not bear the searching eagerness of that wistful gaze, and turning from her answered "can you doubt it you silly little thing, come, take the lamp and go to bed, while I get you something to stop this shivering—he turned to go.

"Do not leave me, oh Louis, stay," she cried, and fell senseless on the floor.

Through that night and for many long days and nights, Natalie lay in a burning fever, and in the delirium caused by it she would beseech him to love her, and again and again in the most pathetic manner entreat him not to leave her, and say, it was very wicked of him not to love her, why was it, what had she done to displease him, then murmur incoherent words about a hateful girl, beautiful but poor that he loved, but not his poor little Natalie, and then starting up with outstretched arms she would implore him to be kind to her and love her.

Whether Louis felt any remorse at dooming a being so bright and fair to such a miserable existence, or whether there was not more anger than sorrow in that impenetrable calm none could tell; he was very attentive, and tried to sooth with gentle words, but woe to any of the attendants who dared to make any remark upon her in his hearing; all she said was treated indifferently as the natural result of the disease, and the nurse was commanded to be silent, when she presumed to say poor dear; whatever passed amongst themselves, in his presence they maintained a discreet silence. When Natalie recovered she was sweet and gentle as ever, but a passive lasting melancholy took the place of her former charming vivacity, henceforth life had lost its charm; with patient love she bore with Louis's variable temper, and was never known to speak a harsh word to little Isabel.

CHAPTER XVIII

Swiftly passed the happy days in the beautiful villa home to which Arthur Barrington had taken his bride. But at length remorseful thoughts of his father's loneliness would intrude themselves upon Arthur's happiest hours, until he could bear it no longer; so he told Louisa the unkind way in which he had left his father, and how unhappy he was on that account, proposing that they should proceed to Barrington Park without delay. To this she readily agreed, but unfortunately their route lay through a district where a malignant fever was very prevalent, and while traversing a lone and dreary portion of this district, Arthur was attacked with this terrible disease. He strove bravely against it, and endeavored to push on to the nearest town, but that was yet forty miles distant, when Arthur became so alarmingly ill that they were forced to stop at a little hamlet and put up with the best accommodation its miserable inn afforded, which was poor indeed. There was no doctor to be had nearer than Z—, but the driver promised to procure one from there if possible. With this they were obliged to be content; but day after day passed and none came, while Arthur hourly became worse, and Louisa grew half wild with grief and fear.

"If we could only get a doctor, I believe he would soon be well; but, ah! it is so dreadful to see him die for want of proper advice," murmured Louisa, glancing toward the bed where Arthur lay tossing in the terrible malaria fever, so fatal to temperaments such as his; "but he will not die, O no I cannot believe that my happiness will be of such short duration that I shall again be left in such icy desolation. Oh! Arthur, Arthur, do not leave me she sobbed, covering her face with her hands, but Arthur does not heed her, racked with burning fever he cannot even recognize her, as with patient gentleness she endeavors to alleviate his sufferings with cooling drinks, or bathes his burning brow. In vain were all the remedies that the simple people of the inn could suggest, or that Louisa's love could devise. Day by day his life ebbed away consumed by the disease, the prostration and langour following the fever being too much for his strength, thus Louisa saw that he who alone in the wide world loved or cared for her, was fast passing away; still though she could not but see it was so, she would not believe the terrible truth, but clung to the hope that a doctor might yet arrive before it was too late, and so her great bereavement came upon her with overwhelming force, when after a day of more than usual langour, during her midnight vigil, he ceased to breathe. Louisa had not known why he had clasped her hand so tightly all that night as she sat beside his couch, he was dead, and with a cry of anguish Louisa fell insensible beside the lifeless body of her husband.

The moonbeams fell alike upon the inanimate forms of the living and the dead, and the morning sun rose brightly and she still lay there, none heard the midnight cry of anguish, or if heard it was unheeded, and the noisy lamentations of the girl who brought in the morning meal, greeted her as consciousness returned. The master of the inn said the funeral must take place at sunset, and Louisa shed bitter tears in the little room which was given her, while the corpse was being prepared for interment, for these precipitate funeral arrangements added greatly to Louisa's grief. Composed but deadly pale she followed Arthur's remains to the grave—his

Clotilda Jennings

only mourner; there was no minister to be had, but Louisa could not see him buried thus, so read herself a portion of the beautiful burial service of the Episcopal Church, then amid tears and sobs she watched them pile and smooth the earth above him, and when they had finished, with a wail of agony she threw herself in a burst of passionate grief upon the damp earth, and there she lay until darkness enveloped all around, heedless of danger, of time, of everything but her deep deep grief, her misery, and her irreparable loss. And there she would have remained but for Francesca, the girl who had waited on them; Francesca had some pity for the poor lady, and with a great effort stifled her superstitious fears, and went down to the grave and led her away, whispering you will get the fever here. So Louisa returned desolate indeed to the miserable inn, not for a moment because of the fear of fever, only dreamily, scarcely knowing where she was going.

Those long hours with the dead had but too surely done their work, Louisa was attacked with the same fever of which her husband died, but carelessly tended and neglected as she was, she did not die.

When she was able to go out again, she would sit pensively for hours by Arthur's grave, or in passionate grief throw herself upon it and wish that she too might die. It was after one of these paroxysms of despair that Louisa remembered her promise to Arthur, that she would take his letter to his father at Barrington Park. Faithful to her word she reluctantly prepared to depart, when to her dismay she found that a cheque for a large amount had been abstracted from Arthur's desk, and further search discovered that nearly every article of value had been perloined during her illness. Their charges were so exorbitant, that it took nearly all the money she had to satisfy their demands, and when she mentioned the cheque, &c., they held up their hands in horror at the idea, that after all their kindness she should suspect them of such villiany.

Weary and broken-hearted, Louisa set out on her lonely journey, and at length arrived sad and dejected at Barrington Park, having had to part with nearly all she possessed in order to prosecute her journey. After some difficulty she succeeded in gaining Lord Barrington's presence.

"Well, what is it you want?" asked his lordship impatiently, but Louisa could not speak, she could only hold out Arthur's letter with a mute gesture of entreaty.

"I don't want to read any of that nonsense; just tell me what you want, and be quick, as I am busy."

Tell him what she wanted!—tell him that she wanted him to love and receive her as a daughter—tell him that the love he bore his son was henceforth to be transferred to the unhappy being before him—how could she tell him this? how could she tell him what she wanted?

"Speak, girl, I say!" he cried, angrily.

"Read this," she faltered, "it will tell you all."

"I will not," he answered; "tell me, or begone!"

Falling on her knees before him, she held out the letter, crying: "I am Arthur's wife. He is dead, and this is his letter, and I am here according to his wish—to his dying injuction. Take it—read it—it will tell you all."

"Good gracious, the girl is mad!" he exclaimed, "mad as a March hare. Come, come! get up and go about your business, or I shall have you put in the asylum."

Clotilda Jennings

Louisa felt choking, she could not speak; she could only stretch out her arms imploringly, still holding the letter.

"There is some great mistake; my son is not dead, nor is he married, so do not think to impose upon me."

"There is no mistake; Arthur is dead, and you see his widow before you," she managed to articulate.

"No, no, Arthur is not dead, poor crazy girl; get up and go away," and he threw her half a sovereign, saying, as he did so, "now go away quickly, or I shall have you turned out; and mind, don't go about with your tale about being my son's wife, or I shall send the police after you. Now go."

Crushed and humbled as she was by sorrow and suffering, this was more than Louisa's fiery nature could endure passively. Springing to her feet, her lips quivering with anger, while her large eyes flashed with passion, she cried, as she threw the proffered alms upon the table, in proud defiance, "Keep your alms for the first beggar you see, but do not insult me. I ask but what is right—that, as your son's wife, I should receive a home and the necessaries of life from you, his father, as he promised me. This you refuse me; but, were I to starve, I would not take your alms, thrown to me as a crazy beggar—never, never!"

"Go, go!" he cried, she by her burst of passionate indignation still more confirming the idea that she was mad.

"I will go," she answered, "and will never again trouble you; but know that I am no impostor—no insane person."

John, who answered his master's summons, stood wonderingly at the door, and, as Louisa passed out, he opened the hall door, looking terribly mystified. "Take this," she said to him, "and if you loved your young master, give this to his father when he will receive it." Then with a full heart Louisa hastened from the park.

A short distance from the gate was a small copse wood, which Louisa entered, and, throwing herself down on the grassy bank beside a stream, gave way to a storm of passionate grief. "Oh, Arthur, Arthur!" she sobbed, "how desolate is Louisa in this cold, cruel world." The storm of grief would have its way, nor did she strive to check it, but continued sobbing convulsively, and shivered with cold, though it was a balmy autumn day; the icy chill at her heart seemed to affect her body also. When at length she became more calm, she began to consider what course she should next pursue. She turned out her scanty store of money—fifteen and sixpence was the whole amount. She determined to return to the inn, where she had left the small bag (the sole remnant of the numerous trunks, etc., with which they had left—), and remain there that night, and start next day for Brierley, the present abode of her grandfather, and try her luck in that quarter, but with small hope of success. Not for herself would she have done this, for she trembled at the thought of meeting him, but circumstances made it imperative.

CHAPTER XIX

"Please maam, is baby to go for her walk this morning," asked the nurse as Louis and Natalie sat at breakfast, "Oh no Sarah," returned Natalie.

"Why not, I should like to know," interposed Louis, "it is a beautiful day and will do her good, I can't see how it is that you always set your face against her going out."

"Oh but Louis, you know she has a bad cold."

"Well it will do her cold good, I can't think where you got the idea, that going out is bad for a cold. Take her out Sarah."

"But Louis I'm afraid it will rain."

"Rain, nonsense, what are you dreaming of this bright morning, take her out by all means Sarah, it will do her good."

Natalie gazed uneasily at the dark storm cloud in the horizon and was anything but satisfied.

"Why Natie you look as sober as a judge" said Louis as he rose to go on his morning calls, "looking out for rain eh, don't be alarmed baby is not sugar nor salt."

The careless gaiety of his tone jarred unpleasantly with her anxious fears for her darling, and she sighed as she looked pensively out upon the bright landscape, with another sigh she left the window and went about her various duties, about an hour after this, Natalie was startled by a vivid flash of lightning, and deafening peal of thunder; down came the rain in torrents, oh where is baby? how anxiously she watched, peering down the street from the front door, but no sign of Izzie, and how cold the air has turned. She orders a fire to be made in the nursery, and waits impatiently for baby's return. She comes at last, "oh my baby!" Natalie exclaims as she takes in her arms the dripping child, wet to the skin, and white as a sheet, every bit of clothing soaked, saturated. Natalie can not restrain her tears as she removes them, and warms the child before the bright fire, "oh my baby, my baby, my poor little Izzie," she murmured passionately, as she soothed and caressed her pet. Baby was happy now in her fresh clothes, and nestled cosily to her mother. After the thunder shower the weather cleared and all seemed bright and joyous without, but Natalie's heart was heavy, she was still very uneasy about the child, Louis was detained from home the entire day. At night baby became so oppressed in her breathing that Natalie was quite alarmed, oh how anxiously did she listen for Louis return, as she knelt by the child's cot in agony watching her intently.

"Oh if he would but come, why, why, did he send her out. Oh the agony, waiting, watching, yes that is his step at last, she sends message after message, but he comes not, he will come when he has had his dinner she is told. It wrings her heart to leave her darling, even for a moment, but it must be done. Softly she glides to where he sits, and laying her trembling hand upon his arm, says in a husky voice "Louis come now, do not wait a moment longer—baby has the croup" in an instant he was at baby's side.

Natalie's ashy face and the word croup, acted like a talisman.

It was croup, and a very bad attack too, he speedily did what was needful, but not without almost breaking his poor little wife's heart, by his cruel remarks, "you should be more careful of her," he said angrily "ten minutes more, and I could have done nothing for her."

"Oh Louis," (he had been home now nearly a quarter of an hour.)

"There must have been some gross mismanagement and fearful neglect, to bring on such an attack as this, to a child that has never been subject to croup, how she ever got into this state passes my understanding, you have been trying some of you foolish schemes I suppose."

"Oh Louis, you know she was out in all that rain to-day" interposed Natalie meekly.

"What was that for, I should like to know," he asked indignantly "are you tired of her already that you don't take better care of her than that?—Oh Natalie!" Natalie's pale cheek flushed at his injustice, but she made no answer, she only watched little Izzie in fear and trembling, and oh how glad and thankful she was when baby presently was sleeping quietly. But how often afterwards did she dwell upon these cruel words, and shed many bitter tears beside her sleeping darling's cot, oh baby, she would murmur, what more care could I take of you than I always do.

CHAPTER XX

In his superbly furnished library sat Lord Barrington. He had just finished reading a letter that he had taken from his desk. "Strange," he murmured, "very strange, that Arthur has not come yet, nor any letter from him; I can't understand it," and he replaced the letter with a heavy sigh. He then turned to the letters on the table, which he had before cast aside, finding the wished-for one was not among them. "Ha, one from George; perhaps he may have seen him." He reads for a while, then starting from his seat exclaimed "Good Heavens! what is this?" Then reads again:

> Judge my amazement when I came across a rude apology for a tombstone, in a little out-of-the-way grave yard: "To the memory of Arthur, only son of Lord Barrington of Barrington, who died August 8th, 1864." As I had not the remotest idea that he was dead, but was almost daily expecting to find him. I most heartily sympathize with you—

"What can he mean?" he said, putting down the letter. "But what is this?" he cried, as his eye caught one he had overlooked before. 'Tis Arthur's hand!" With trembling hands he broke the seal (taking no note, in his agitation, of the fact that it had not been through the post), and read the almost unintelligible scrawl:

Clotilda Jennings

DEAR FATHER:—I have charged Louisa to bring this and give it into your own hand. She will not believe that I am dying, and still clings to the hope that I will recover. But it can not be; I feel—I know—that I shall die. Oh, how I wish that I could see you again once more and ask your forgiveness, but it may not be! With my dying breath I beseech you to forgive your erring boy; it was the first, it is the last deception I ever practiced toward you. To you I ever confided my hopes and plans, and you always strove to gratify every wish. I feel now how much I wronged your generous nature, when I feared to tell you of my intended marriage. The tune seems ever before me when you asked me, even with tears, why I wished to leave you again, after I returned from America, and I answered, evasively, that I wanted to see the world. And when, in the fullness of your love, you replied "Then I will go with you," I answered angrily, "In that case I do not care to go," and pleaded for just one year. And you granted my request, and sent me forth with blessings. Oh, why did I not tell you all? I feel sure that you would have replied, "Bring your wife home, Arthur, and I will love her as a daughter, only do not leave me." Oh, father, forgive your boy! Thoughts of your loneliness would intrude at all times and mar my happiness, until I determined to return and bring my wife, trusting to your love, and was on my way home when I was attacked with this dreadful fever. Oh, how I repent that I did not mention my wife in my last letter to you! It is but a few short months since I left you, but O how long those lonely months must have been to you! Then let your sad hours be cheered by Louisa, since the sight of your boy may never gladden your heart in this world. Bestow upon her the same love and kindness you have ever shown to me. Nothing can alleviate my pain in leaving her, but the certainty I feel that you will love and cherish her for my sake. Oh make not her coming alone harder by one word or action. But as you love me, so deal with my wife. Farewell, dear father!—a last farewell! Before you receive this, I shall be sleeping in my distant grave. And oh when my poor Louisa presents it, treat her not harshly, as you hope that we shall meet again.

Your affectionate and repentant son,
ARTHUR.

As the old man ceased reading, his head fell upon the table, and bitter tears coursed down his cheeks. "Oh, Arthur! Arthur! my boy! my only child! why, why did you leave me? How gladly would I have received your wife! But now how harshly have I treated her—how cruelly sent her forth into this heartless world, friendless and alone! But I will find her and bring her home—yes, yes, I will love her for his sake. Oh if I had only taken this when she brought it! But I will lose no time now. Oh, Arthur! Arthur!" he murmured, and he rang the bell violently. "John! John!" he said to the faithful old man who answered his summons, "stay, John, till I can speak," he cried, gasping for breath and trembling from head to foot. "My boy, my Arthur is dead!" he wailed, at length, and that person—that lady—was his widow, John. It was all true that she said, and I treated her so badly, too."

"Yes," old John replied, meekly, "I thought it wor true; she didn't look like an himpostor, she didn't," and he shook his head gravely.

"You must find her, John, and bring her back. Go, you have your orders; you must find her. Arthur is dead, and he has sent his wife to me, and I must take care of her—that is all I can do for him now."

"Ah, that's the way with them secret marriages," soliloquized old John. "What in the world made Mr. Arthur act so, I wonder, and his governor so indulgent?"

"Yes we will find her, and she shall have the green room, not Arthur's—no, not Arthur's. Love her for his sake, he says; aye that I will," murmured his lordship, as he paced the room. "Too late, old man, too late, too late."

CHAPTER XXI

"I declare it's a shame," cried Emily throwing a letter on the table. "I can't think what Everard means, it's positively unkind, I shall write and tell him so," she continued endeavoring in vain to repress the tears of vexation that would not be restrained. "I would not have believed it of him, indeed I would not—what will Harry think, I should like to know."

"What is the matter," asked Grace and Isabel at the same time.

"Read this and you will see," she replied—Grace read—

DEAR EMILY,—You will, I know, be sorry to hear that I cannot be home for the Xmas. festivities, nor for the wedding; I am as sorry as you can possibly be, dear Emmy, but circumstances, over which I have no control, make it imperitive that I should remain away, therefore, pray forgive my absence, nor think it unkind.

"It is outrageous" said Grace folding the letter carefully. "Mamma will not allow it I am certain, and I cannot imagine any reason that could prevent him coming if he chose. You had better get mamma or papa to write, people will think it so strange."

"I don't care what people think, it's Harry and ourselves" replied Emily hotly, "I will write and tell him that I won't be married this Xmas. if he don't come—'there.'"

"How absurd" returned Grace contemptuously.

"Do you mean it" inquired Isabel gravely.

"Oh that is another thing" replied Emily coloring, but I shall say so, and try the effect."

"It cannot be his wish to stay away" said Isabel thoughtfully.

"It is the strangest thing I ever knew," replied Grace.

"Isabel felt very uncomfortable, for somehow she could not help thinking that she might be the cause, (as, once, Everard had been very near the forbidden subject, saying that it was quite a punishment to be under the same roof, unless there was some change in their position, toward each other.

"She was sorry that he had not said so before Isabel had replied, and that very day, told Mrs. Arlington that she wished to leave, as soon as she could meet with another governess. Mrs. Arlington asked her reasons. But Miss Leicester would give none. Then Mrs. Arlington requested that Miss Leicester would reconsider the matter, but Miss Leicester refused to do so. Then Mrs. Arlington insisted, saying that she would except her resignation, if at the end of the week she still wished it, though they would all be sorry to part with her.

Everard of course heard what had taken place, and immediately made it his business to alter that young lady's determination, protesting that he had said nothing to make her pursue such a course. He forced her to admit that it was solely on his account that she was leaving, and then talked her into consenting to withdraw her resignation at the end of the week, promising to be more careful not to offend in future.) She wished very much that she could spend this Xmas. with Mrs. Arnold, but this was impossible, as she had promised Emily to be bridesmaid.

"Then you don't think it would do to say that," Emily said inquiringly.

"It would seem childish" returned Isabel.

"And have no effect," added Grace.

"Coaxing would be better you think."

"Decidedly," said Isabel laughing.

"The begging and praying style, might answer" returned Grace scornfully, "he always likes to be made a fuss with, and all that nonsense, if the children do but kiss him, and call him a dear kind brother and such like rubbish, he will do almost anything."

Now Grace don't say the children, when you mean me, interposed Emily, I will not hear a word against Evvie, so don't be cross. I know you always were a little jealous of his partiality for me."

"I am not cross, nor did I say anything against Everard," retorted Grace haughtily "and as for partiality, where is the favouritism now."

"Oh well, I shall write such a letter that he can't but come."

"I wish you success with all my heart," returned Grace more good naturedly, while Isabel gazed silently out of the window.

* * * * * * * *

"No answer to my letter yet, is it not strange said Emily as she joined Isabel in her favourite retreat, the conservatory, "what do you think about it, it makes me positively unhappy."

"Shall I tell you what I think" asked Isabel passing her arm round Emily and continuing her walk.

"Do please, for you can't think how disagreeable it is, when Harry asks, when Everard is coming, to have to give the same stupid answer, I expect to hear every day."

"I don't think you will."

"Oh Isabel."

"No, I do not think he will write, but just quietly walk in one of these days!"

"Do you really think so," asked Emily, her face radiant.

Isabel gave an affirmative nod.

"What makes you think so, Isabel?"

"I don't know, but I feel sure he will," she replied, turning away her face.

"Isabel."

"Well, dear," said Isabel, with heightening color, still

keeping her face turned away, "tell me, was it because of you that Everard would not come home."

"I don't know."

"Then you think, perhaps, it may be."

"It is very foolish to think so."

"Then you do think so," said Emily, archly.

"Oh, miss, I have found you out at last. What a sly one you are. I have been watching you a long time, and thought you all unconscious how it was with a certain party who shall be nameless. Oh I'm so glad."

"Glad that your brother is so unhappy?" Oh, Emily!

"No; glad that he need be so no longer."

"How do you mean?"

"How do I mean! Why how obtuse you are, Isabel."

"You run on too fast."

"Oh, not much. I found out how it was on his part long ago, and I shall not be long before I tell him the result of my observations elsewhere."

"Tell him what?" asked Isabel, aghast,

"To go in and win," replied Emily, saucily.

"Emily, Emily! what are you saying—what do you mean?"

"Mean?" replied Emily, with a saucy nod, "to help on my pet scheme a little, that's all."

"You never mean to say that you intend to—"

"Oh, but I do, though."

"Emily, if you dare!" cried Isabel, indignantly.

"Ah, but I shall."

"You shall not," said Isabel, grasping her arm, "you do not know what you are about."

"Yes I do, perfectly well, and you will both thank me hereafter."

"Stop a moment; what is it you intend to tell him?"

"Only what I have found out—that all is as he wishes, so he need not be afraid."

"You have not found out any such thing."

"Oh, have I not though?"

"Decidedly not. All you have discovered is, that I had some foolish idea that it might possibly be on my account that he was not coming home. That is all you could honestly tell him, and you will do more harm than good if you do; depend upon it, you will only make matters worse by interfering."

"Well, if it is to do no good, I would rather that he did not know I had found out his secret, but keep it as I have done."

"Since when?" asked Isabel.

"Last spring, when we had to leave you on the rock, but of course I did not let him see it."

"Then do not enlighten him now, you will only make him uncomfortable."

"You are right, but come tell me since when did you know."

"I have known a long time."

"But does he think you know."

Isabel was silent.

"Come, miss, how did you find out?"

"Don't, Emily," said Isabel, entreatingly.

"How did you know—did he tell you?"

"Is this generous?" asked Isabel, with burning cheeks."

"You don't mean to say that you refused him?" said Emily, turning her blue eyes full upon Isabel, "that would be too cruel."

"Be quiet, Emily," implored Isabel.

"I see how it is now. Oh, Isabel, how could you?"

"Remember, Emily, I have told you nothing; you have found out my secret; keep it better than you did your brother's."

"Oh, Isabel, I am sure I kept that well enough."

"Not so well as you must keep this. I am very, very sorry, for

I feel that I have not been sufficiently watchful, or you would I not have suspected it. And he would be justly angry if he knew."

"Well, under the circumstances it would make no difference to you if he was."

Isabel bit her lip and was silent, then said, "Emily, dear Emily, promise me that you will try to forget this conversation, and never mention it to any one."

"But Isabel when was it."

"I will answer no questions on that subject" more than enough has been said already.

"What a rage Grace would be in, if she knew, well, well, I have my own ideas."

"Have you indeed, and pray what would Grace be in a rage about if she knew," asked a well known voice close to them.

Both young ladies started and crimsoned. "You see Emmy I could not resist that letter, so here I am for a few days."

"Isabel was right" cried Emily triumphantly, "she said you would come quietly in, one of these days."

"What made you think so," he asked.

"I felt sure of it, I cannot tell why, but I had a presentiment that you would."

"May I hope that the wish was the origin of the thought," he said in a low tone, as Emily turned to caress his dog, Hector.

"Certainly" she answered laughing. "I would not have Emily disappointed on any account."

"Such a true prophet ought to be rewarded, don't you think so Emily," said Everard presenting Isabel with the first and only flower of a rare foreign plant.

"I cannot accept it," replied Isabel, "the reward is more than the prediction was worth."

"Oh no, it is not, I am sure you earned it," cried Emily clapping her hands, and running off with Hector for a romp.

"Surely you will not refuse a flower" said Everard.

"But why that flower."

"Because it is the best."

"For that very reason, I cannot accept it."

"You are over scrupulous Miss Leicester."

"No, only prudent."

He looked hurt, "you will not refuse" he urged.

"I dare not accept it."

"Why."

"What would they think."

"If the truth,—, that the flower I valued most, I gave to the one I loved best."

"Are you not venturing on forbidden grounds" asked Isabel with glowing cheeks.

"Isabel you are cruel."

"I do not wish to pain you."

"Then accept my flower."

"No, were I to do so, I could only take it to your mother saying that you wished it preserved."

"Would you do so Isabel," he exclaimed reproachfully.

"I should be obliged to do so, if I took it."

"Is it only this one you refuse."

"Or any other equally valuable and scarce."

Gathering a choice little bouquet he said "you will not refuse this Isabel."

"Miss Leicester if you please sir," she replied as she took the flowers, and hastened to the schoolroom. While Everard stood for a moment lost in thought, then went to pay his respects to his mother, and present the rejected flower, to the bride elect.

This was the last evening they would be alone, to-morrow the guests were to arrive. Isabel did not always join them at dinner, and this evening she intended to spend in the school-room to finish the reports, which Mr. Arlington always liked to have when the holidays began, giving the children leave to go in the drawing-room. But the best plans cannot always be carried out. Isabel received a message from Mrs. Arlington requesting her to join them at dinner, accompanied by a threat from Harry, that if she did not they would all adjourn to the schoolroom, of course she had to comply. However the evening passed off very pleasantly, Everard was so much occupied with his mother and sisters, that with the exception of making her sing all his favourite songs, he paid even less than usual attention to Isabel.

CHAPTER XXII

The children are on tiptoe of expectation, anxiously waiting the arrival of the Mornington's, and numerous other guest's. Now the wished for moment has come, what a delightful stir and confusion it has occasioned. Rose is in ecstasy, and Amy wild with glee, even the quiet Alice seemed to have caught the infection. It was to be a regular old fashioned Xmas. Eve. All sorts of games and odd things, snap dragon, charades (for which Harry and Lucy were famous) magic music, dancing, and even blindmans buff was proposed but was over-ruled by the quieter members of the party. 'Santa Claus' sent a bountiful supply of presents down the chimney that night, which caused great merriment next day. For ladies got smoking caps, and cigar-cases; while gentlemen received workboxes, thimbles, and tatting-needles. Peter got a jester's cap and bells, which he vowed was a dunce's cap intended for Rose, to that young lady's great indignation. Tom had a primer, and a present for a good boy, and May received a plain gold ring at which they all laughed very much, to May's excessive annoyance. After breakfast they all went to church, and then all who chose went to see the school children, who were enjoying themselves immensely over their Xmas. fare. Then the sleighs were had out for a glorious drive over the frozen snow, but Isabel refused to join the party, preferring to stay quietly at home. To practise anthem's with Everard, Grace said. Isabel had no such idea, but for all that they did sing some anthems with the children, as Everard, who had taken a very active part in the arrangements for the Sunday School feast, was not of course one of the sleighing party, and returned some time before them. The children sang very nicely, doing great credit to Isabel's teaching, for which she was highly complimented by Everard.

"They ought to be much obliged to you, as they bid fair to surpass both Grace and Emily," he said.

"Pray don't let Miss Arlington hear you say so, or she will never forgive me."

"Oh never fear, she would not believe it, but I will be careful, as she is already dreadfully jealous of you."

"Of me, how can she be, why should she."

"She has cause enough," he replied warmly, "but she should be more magnanimous."

"I don't think it possible, I cannot imagine she could be so silly."

"It is plain enough to me, that she is."

"I don't see it, I confess."

"'Where ignorance is bliss,' he replied, with one of his usual penetrating glances. "Yours must be a very happily constituted mind to be so unconscious of all things disagreeable."

"Not quite so unconscious as you imagine, but I advise you not to fish into troubled waters."

"Still waters run deep, you mean," he replied.

"Unfathomable," she said, and followed the children to the dining-room, for they had gone there to see if the decorations were completed. A right merry party sat down to dinner, sixty in number, all relations or old friends. Here is Tom's description of the wedding nest day, which he sent his friend:

DEAR DICK,—We are having jolly times here—rare fun on Christmas-eve, I assure you. But the best of all was my brother's wedding; eight bridesmaids, all as beautiful as sunshine. (I was a best-man, of course.) The bride looked magnificent—(between you and I, Dick, he has made a very good choice)—the rain and sunshine style. I can't say I understand that kind of thing, but on such occasions it tells immensely. (I admire one of the bridesmaids amazingly, but mum's the word, mind.) But to speak of the wedding. Governor Arlington is a liberal old fellow. Champagne like water, and everything to match.

Your's truly, T. M.

Elm Grove was scarcely the same place to Isabel when Emily was gone. She toiled on diligently with the children, but she found teaching anything but pleasant. Often after a tedious day, when tired and weary, she would gladly have laid down to rest her aching head and throbbing temples. Mrs. Arlington would request that she would join them in the drawing-room. Isabel did not consider herself at liberty to refuse, besides she did not wish to encounter Mrs. Arlington's frowns next day; and even when they were out, and she congratulated herself upon being left in peace, Mr. Arlington (who seldom accompanied hem) would ask her to sing some songs, or play a game of chess, and of course she had to comply. This kind of life was very irksome to Isabel—so different to what she had been accustomed to.

She strove bravely with her fate, but in spite of all her endeavors she often cried herself to sleep she felt so desolate and alone. She had no home: there was no hearth where she was missed, or her coming anxiously looked for. Then she would grieve bitterly over the bright home she had lost, and the happy days gone, it seemed, for ever; and then in the morning be angry with herself for her ingratitude, remembering the blessings she still enjoyed, and how much worse off she might be, and strive to be contented. A fresh cause for disquietude arose, Grace evidently was jealous of her. Grace was handsome, but she was aware that Isabel was more attractive. Grace sang well, but she also knew that Isabel sang better, her voice was richer, fuller, more melodious. She said that Isabel always wanted to show off, and would look very incredulous and neutral when Isabel's performances were praised. One gentleman in particular was very enthusiastic in his praises. "But professional people are different you know," returned Grace.

"Oh indeed, I was not aware that Miss Leicester was a professional singer," he replied.

"Not a professional singer, she teaches singing," said Grace thinking she was going a little too far.

"Indeed, where did you make her acquaintance, may I ask, you seldom hear such a splendid voice."

"Oh she is our governess," replied Grace.

Turning to Isabel he said "you have a very fine voice Miss Leicester, if you were to make your debut at one of our best operas, you would make your fortune."

"I have no such idea," said Isabel, the indignant tears starting to her eyes, "that is the last thing I should thing of doing, she added with a reproachful look at Grace," but Grace seemed to be enjoying the whole thing amazingly.

"I do not suppose that you have thought of it or you certainly would not be a governess, with such a career open to you; with very little training you might command almost any salary." Isabel was excessively annoyed. "I assure you my dear young lady that it is worth your consideration he continued.

"You mean well, no doubt, Mr. Bandolf, and I thank you for your kind intentions; but the matter requires no consideration, I could not entertain the idea for a moment" returned Isabel, and bowing coldly opened a book of prints.

"You should not let pride prevent your worldly advancement," he added, which only made her more angry than ever. For all this I have to thank Miss Arlington she thought, and her feelings toward that young lady, at that moment, were not the most charitable.

CHAPTER XXIII

"No I am sure it never answers at least not in most cases and in ours it would not I am convinced; but I had a pretty hard battle about it I assure you Ada."

"I had no idea until now that they wished it" returned Ada. "but I am very glad you did not agree to it."

(The matter under consideration was, if it were desirable that young couples should reside with the parents of either; but Charles Ashton knew his mother's disposition too well, to subject his wife to it, though he was a very good son and loved his mother. He had no wish, nor did he consider himself at liberty to place his wife in a position that he knew might make her very unhappy. Nor did he think that such an arrangement would promote domestic bliss. He was a particularly quiet easy going fellow, very averse to exertion of any kind and seldom troubled himself to oppose any arrangements, usually agreeing to any proposition for the sake of peace and quietness. But for all that he had a will of his own, and when he had once made up his mind, nothing on earth could move him. Before he married he gave the matter careful considertion, and came to the conclusion that it must never be—never Ada would be his wife, and no mortal should breathe a word against her in his hearing— therefore it must never be. Having come to this conclusion he waited until the subject should be broached by either of his parents, knowing very well that when that topic should be discussed, then would come the tug of war, and he was not at all anxious for it. It soon came however, his father proposed that he should bring his bride there, saying, "there is plenty of room for all." But Charles was not so sure of that, and feared that the house might possibly become too hot to hold them, but merely stated quietly that he had decided otherwise. Then arose a perfect storm, but he was firm. His mother asked with her handkerchief to her eyes, if she was to lose her boy altogether. While Lord Ashton requested to be informed what his plans might be.

"To live in England" he answered.

"What might be his objection to Ashton Park."

He had nothing to say against Ashton Park, but he wished to reside in England.

Very well, they would go to England, and all live together, that would be charming Lady Ashton said.

"He should like them to live in England, but as to living together, that was out of the question," Charles replied.

"Whereupon Lady Ashton was highly offended and very angry. Charles was quiet, but firm, all they could urge was useless, he would not hear of it.) "It might answer in Arthur's case" he returned, by the way Ada is it not strange we have never heard anything of them, poor Louisa, I suppose boarding school did not answer her expectations, as she left it so soon."

"Can you wonder at it, situated as she was."

"It was natural no doubt, and Arthur could be so winning, he always was a favourite with the ladies."

"Oh well, he is a nice fellow you must admit."

"I don't deny it, I always liked him very much, but still I think that sort of thing, is not right, but he always was impetuous, never considered anything, but just acted on the spur of the moment, and he is very soft hearted" he added laughing. "I wonder if the old gentleman knows it."

"Your mother was always ambitious for him, don't you remember how afraid she was about Isabel" asked Ada.

"Yes, and the daughter of his tutor does not come up to the mark."

"I should think her own daughter's child might at all events."

"But she never regards her in that light, never will I fear."

"Somebody wishes to see you Sir, very particularly please," said Thomson.

"Who is it? Thomson."

"Don't know I'm sure Sir, she would not give any name, but is very anxious to see you, I said you were engaged, but she replied I that she must see you to-night, it was very important."

"What sort of a person is she?" asked Ada.

"A lady madam, quite a lady I should say, only in trouble, she says she knew master in America."

"I must see her, I suppose, where is she."

"In the study, sir."

The stranger was standing by the fire-place, as he entered she made an impatient gesture for him to close the door, then threw herself at his feet passionately imploring him to help and protect her, and throwing aside her thick vail, disclosed the features of Louisa, but so altered that he was perfectly shocked and amazed. He could scarcely believe that the haggered emaciated being before him, was indeed the pretty, impulsive, fiery, Louisa, but such was the case, and anger, compassion and indignation filled his heart, as he listened to the recital of her misfortunes.

As the reader is already acquainted with a portion of Louisa's story, we will not repeat it here, but only record such circumstances as have not appeared in these pages. On arriving at her grandfather's she encountered a storm of angry abuse, and was driven from the door with a stern command never to return, as she had forfeited all claims upon him, and might die in a ditch for all he cared. She managed to get about a mile from the house, and then overcome with fatigue and misery she sank down exhausted.

How long she remained there she had no idea, when she recovered she was among strangers, who were very kind. She had had a brain fever, and was in the hospital When asked for the address of her friends, she replied that she had none. But afterward she remembered that her Uncle Charles had always been kind to her, and had occasionally procured her little indulgences from her stern, cold-hearted, grandmother, and that it had been mainly through his interference that she had been sent to school. She therefore determined to seek his aid, and accept a small loan from the doctor, to enable her to do so, long and weary had the journey been, and she implored Charles not to send her away. She knew she said that it would not be for long, and entreated him to let her die in peace.

Charles assured her that she should want for nothing, and commended her for coming to him, and expressed in no measured terms his disapprobation of his father's cruel conduct, but was abruptly silenced by Louisa falling senseless on the floor. His violent ringing of the bell, brought not only the servants, but Ada also, to his assistance; medical aid was quickly procured. That night her child was born, and when morning dawned, Louisa lay still and cold in that last long sleep from which no mortal could awake her. Sleep in thy marble beauty, poor little Louisa, and perhaps that sad fate may soften the hearts of thy cruel grandparent. Oh not as it has been fulfilled did the dying Evangeline understand the promise made with regard to the little Louisa. Oh how often was the stillness of the night broken by the bitter sobs of the desolate little orphan whose aching heart sought for love in vain. Then can we wonder that when this lonely one, did find one to love, that she should willingly listen to his persuasions in hopes of a happy future, rather than endure any longer such a cheerless existence.

In the early morning a violent knocking at the hall door brought Thomson from his gossip with the other servants.

"Is there not a lady—a widow lady, staying here?" inquired an old gentleman in an agitated voice, while the cab driver beat his arms on the pavement. "Is not this Mr. Ashton's?" he added, as Thomson hesitated. Thomson answered in the affirmative, and the old gentleman continued, "Is the lady here? Can I see your master? answer me quickly don't be so stupid."

"A lady came last night but, but," stammered Thomson "she,"

"Is she here now, I say," he cried angrily.

"Yes sir, but—

"Say no more, just tell your master I want to see him immediately, stop, take my card, here, now be quick."

Poor Thomas was quite bewildered by the old gentleman's manner. I'm blest he murmured if I know what we're coming to next, Lord Barrington, what does he want I should like to know.

"Why Ada, it is Lord Barrington," exclaimed Charles.

"How very fortunate," returned Ada "of course he will take charge of the baby, I confess I was in a quandary for I do not relish the idea of having the care of it, poor little thing."

"Nor I either, but I am not so sure that he will take it, it is much more likely he has come to row me about the whole affair."

"You! Why, what had you to do with it?"

"No more than you had; but I must see him at once, I suppose."

"Shall I go, too?" asked Ada, timidly.

"Not at present: if there is to be a storm, I do not see why you should be in it."

"He is such a dreadful old man, is he not?"

"Not usually; he was always very, very kind to Arthur."

"Not to his wife," she replied, vainly endeavoring to repress her tears.

"No, very cruel; but you must not grieve so much about it, dearest Ada."

"I cannot help it, it is so terribly shocking."

"But it is past, now: she is at rest, she is happy; even her lifeless remains look calm—the weary, weary look exchanged for one of peace."

"True, but it is so dreadful; if we had only known before," she sobbed.

"I wish we had, with all my soul," returned Charles, "but you really must not distress yourself so, or I shall have to keep the poor old gent waiting."

"Go to him, Charley; I shall feel better presently."

He found his Lordship impatiently pacing the room. "I am seeking my daughter-in-law; she is here, I believe," he said, after the first salutations were over.

"She is here," Charles answered gravely, "at least her remains; she died last night."

"Dead! dead!" repeated Lord Barrington, putting his hand to his head. "Then I have nothing left."

"But the child," interposed Charles.

"The child—what child?"

Clotilda Jennings

"The babe born last night."

"He did not heed the answer, but seemed overpowered by the news of Louisa's death. "Let me see Arthur's wife," he said, after a few minutes had elapsed. Charles conducted him to the darkened apartment, where he gazed in agony upon the worn, but calm features of poor Louisa. And as he thought of his harshness, and Arthur's words, "make not her coming alone harder by one word or look," his grief became so violent and excessive that Charles was quite nonplussed, and went to consult Ada as to what should be done. In accordance with their plan, Ada took the frail little piece of humanity, and, approaching Lord Barrington, as he bent in sorrow over the corpse, said softly, "You have lost Arthur, and Arthur's wife, but you still have Arthur's child," and she laid the babe in his arms.

His tears fell on its tiny face, but the sight of it, and its helplessness, did him good. "Oh, Arthur! Arthur!" he moaned, why did you doubt your old father? how would I have welcomed your wife if you had brought her home at first! aye, as I now welcome this child—Arthur's child," he added, looking at it fondly.

He had the corpse conveyed to Barrington, and placed in the family vault, and erected a monument—very beautiful, indeed—beside the one he had already placed there in memory of his son, inscribed:

To
LOUISA,
the beloved wife of Arthur,
only son of
LORD BARRINGTON OF BARRINGTON,
Aged 16 years.

He also placed another in the little burying-place at Z—:

In memory of
ARTHUR,
only son of LORD BARRINGTON, of Barrington Park,
England,
aged 23 years,
who was suddenly attacked with a fatal fever,
in a foreign land,
when on his way home.

When Lady Ashton arrived, shortly afterwards, and heard what had taken place, she was in a terrible fume. "Oh! my dear, what a misfortune. How unlucky for her to come here: why did you let her stay, Charles?"

"Why did I let her stay? Say, rather, why did you send her away?"

"Yes, why did you let her stay?" she repeated, angrily. "Why did you not let her go to the hospital?"

"Or die in the street," added Charles, scarcely able to keep his temper, for he was angry and hurt to think how Louisa had been treated.

"Goodness knows what people will say: no doubt all kinds of strange stories will be circulated. I feel for you, Ada, my dear; I do, indeed."

"Don't be alarmed, my dear mother, as to rumors and strange stories," said Charles, handing her a newspaper, and pointing out the following:

DIED.—At the residence of Charles Ashton, Esq. LOUISA, wife of the late Hon. Arthur Barrington, and

Clotilda Jennings

grand-daughter of Sir Edward Ashton of Brierley.

"Charles, how dared you?" cried his mother, reddening with anger, "your father will be excessively angry."

"I cannot help that: it is the truth, is it not?"

"True? of course you know it is; but, for all that, you need not have published it in that absurd manner."

"I thought it best."

"And you are simple enough to think that that notice will prevent absurd stories getting abroad."

"As to who she might be, yes; and, as to the circumstances that brought her here, I presume you would prefer any, rather than the right ones, should be assigned."

Lady Ashton was for once abashed, and her eye dropped beneath the severity of her son's gaze; but, recovering quickly, she answered, "you, at least, have nothing to do with that."

"I am thankful to say I have not," he returned, "I cannot forget it, it makes me perfectly wretched; and, but that I know that Ada has her own home to go to, if anything happened to me I don't know what I should do. I shall insure my life this very day, that she may be independent. If a daughter's child could be so treated, why not a son's wife."

For goodness' sake stop, Charles!" cried his mother, "don't talk so dreadfully."

"I feel it bitterly, mother; indeed I do," he replied, and hastily left the room. He would not have done so, however, had he known the storm he had left Ada to be the unhappy recipient of. She was perfectly terrified at the violence of Lady Ashton's wrath, and Lady Ashton was, too, when she saw Ada lay back in her chair, pale as marble and panting for breath. "What is the matter?—speak, child," she cried, shaking her violently; but this only alarmed her the more, and she called loudly for Charles, and then remained gazing at Lady Ashton in speechless terror.

"Ada! dearest Ada! what is the matter?" asked Charles, coming to the rescue; but Ada had fainted.

CHAPTER XXIV

"Well, old fellow, how are you?" said Louis, as he entered Everard's room at the college. "I only just heard you were back." After they had conversed awhile, Louis said, "Pretty girl that governess your sisters have at Elm Grove; aye, only she is such a confounded flirt."

"I esteem Miss Leicester very highly," returned Everard, coldly.

"Take care, old fellow, for she is, without exception, the greatest coquette I ever came across. She always had crowds of admirers, many of whom she contrived to draw on until they came to 'the point,' and then laughed at them. By Jove she will make a fool of you, Everard, if you don't mind."

"I assure you, Louis, that you are quite mistaken. Miss Leicester is quite a different person to what you imagine."

"Ha! ha! so you may think, but I knew her intimately, and I must say that I was surprised that your mother should trust her young daughters to her care."

"Be quiet, Louis; I think her as near perfection as possible."

"Well, they say that love is blind—stone blind, in this case, I should say. She must have played her game well, to deceive you so thoroughly."

"I am not deceived, neither has she played any game," returned Everard, with warmth. "She gives me no encouragement whatever—very far from it."

"Oh, that is her new dodge, is it? Beware of her; she is a most accomplished actress."

"You are mistaken," replied Everard, indignantly, "you know some one else of the same name."

"Not a bit of it, my dear fellow; I saw the young minx at Elm Grove, and knew her directly. 'Beautiful, but dangerous.' I know her well."

Everard's cheek flushed with anger. "Louis," said he, "I will not hear any one speak disrespectfully of Miss Leicester. I consider any insult offered to her as a personal affront; therefore, if we are to remain friends, you must say no more on that subject now or at any other time."

Louis saw by Everard's countenance that he was in earnest, so answered, "as you will. I have satisfied my conscience by warning you; of course I can do no more. Won't you dine with us to-day?"

"No, really, I cannot possibly; I have no time to go anywhere."

"Take care you don't work too hard, and have to give up altogether. You look as if you were overdoing it. Too much of a good thing is good for nothing, you know. Come when you can—if not to-day, I shall be always glad to see you."

"What object can he have in speaking thus of Isabel?" Everard asked himself when Louis was gone—his beautiful and beloved Isabel, the charm of his existence, yet the torture of his life—(for was it not torture to be forever dwelling on her perfections, only to come back to the same undeniable fact that she had refused him—that she either could not, or would not, be his)—and now to hear *her*, the personification of his own ideal, spoken of as an accomplished actress and deceitful coquette, was almost more than he could endure. Then he asked himself what he had gained by his constant and excessive study: had it caused him to forget her? no, he could not forget she seemed ever with him in all her beauty, gentleness, and truth. He would win her yet, he told himself, and then owned he was a fool to indulge such thoughts, and determined to study harder still than ever, to prevent the possibility of his thoughts recurring so often to Isabel. Nevertheless, he would believe nothing against her— nothing.

CHAPTER XXV

"Louis, I wish you would look at baby before you go; I do not think she is well to-night."

"What is the matter now? You are always thinking she is ill: she seemed well enough this morning."

"I don't know. She is restless and uneasy; I wish you would come."

"Of course I will, but I am in a great hurry just now; Mrs. Headley has sent for me, and old Mr. Growl has another attack. I must go to the people in the office now, but I will come up to baby before I start."

"Had you not better see baby first? Perhaps you might forget, with so many people to attend to."

"Forget? Not I. Why, Natalie, how do you think I should ever get on if I had no better memory than that?"

But he did forget, and was gone when Natalie again sought him. "I thought it would be so," she sighed. Baby became more and more uneasy, and moaned and fretted in her sleep. Natalie knelt beside the bed, and tried to soothe her darling, thinking sadly of the long hours that would elapse before

Louis's return, but all her efforts were in vain. Izzie did not wake or cry, but this only alarmed Natalie the more. The deadly palor of her countenance was the only sign of the anguish she suffered; outwardly, she was very calm. If she could only have done anything for her pet! but to wait, and watch, not knowing what to do, this was unendurable; and she was just debating in her own mind if she ought not to send for another doctor, as Louis might be detained all night, when she heard him come in. She pressed her cold hands upon her brow, and ordered Sarah to bring him immediately; while she rose from her knees, and breathlessly waited for his coming.

"What's the matter with popsy?" he asked, cheerfully, as he entered the room, but his countenance became grave as his eye rested on the sick child. "What is this?," he inquired, "why was I not told before? Tut, tut, what have you been thinking about, Natalie," he added, as he felt the child's pulse.

"I asked you to come and see her before you went out," Natalie answered, in an almost inaudible voice.

"Yes, but you did not say that there was anything particularly the matter." He stooped over the child and examined her more carefully. "She is seriously ill," he said.

And the words sent a thrill of pain to Natalie's aching heart.

"Why do you treat me in this shameful manner?" he continued bitterly. "Why let the child go on until it is almost past recovery, and then send for me in the greatest haste?— just the same way when she had the croup. I am surprised at you Natalie; it is really quite childish." He ordered the bath to be brought immediately.

Impatiently waving Natalie aside, he took the child in his arms and put her into the bath; while Natalie stood by, in speechless agony, Louis refusing to allow her to assist in any way. How cruel! To have done anything for her darling would have been an unspeakable relief. As it was, she could only stand by while he murmured, in a tone which greatly distressed her "poor little popsy," "Did they neglect papa's darling?" He would suffer no one to touch her but himself, and what assistance he did accept was from Sarah, it being into her arms he put baby while he went for the medicine she required. Poor Natalie, how this grieved her; for though she took the child from Sarah, the slight was the same. "Oh, baby, baby!" she murmured, as the burning tears fell on little Isabel's face, "what should I have left if you were taken from me?"

When Louis returned, he took the child, administered the medicine, and was about to lay her in the bed.

"Let me take her," whispered Natalie, in a tone of tremulous earnestness and passionate entreaty.

"No, she is better here," he replied.

"Oh, please, Louis!" she pleaded, but he was firm.

She stood, with clasped hands, silently gazing on the babe with a strange sensation of awe and dread, and a yearning wish to do something for her.

"You are not required, Natalie," Louis said, "you had better go to bed." With a gulp she restrained the rising sob, and stooped to kiss her darling. "You will only disturb her," he said, putting out his arm to prevent her doing so. Then Natalie could only steal away to her dressing-room, and there, alone in the darkness, she crept to the sofa and hid her

Clotilda Jennings

face in the cushion, to hush the tumultuous sobs, while she breathed fervent prayers for baby's recovery. But a horrible dread surrounded her: she could not endure to be absent from her pet, and noiselessly she stole back to the nursery. She was glad that Louis did not observe her entrance, and retreated to the dimmest corner of the room, and there, in the old arm-chair, listened to baby's uneasy breathing, which caused her an agony of grief and pain. Yet she could do nothing but sit and suffer—suffer, oh, how deeply! Thus the night wore away, and Louis was not aware of her presence until, as the day dawned, he beheld the wan, wretched face of his poor little wife. Going to her side, he said, "this is wrong, Natalie; go and rest." She shook her head. "You must, indeed: you know I have to leave her to you the greater part of the day, and this is no preparation for the watchful care she will need."

"She cannot need more care than I will gladly give," returned Natalie, with trembling lip. Her face wore an expression, so sad—so suffering—that Louis must, indeed, have been adamant if he had not been softened. Stroking her hair caressingly, he was about to lead her from the room with gentle force, when, grasping his hand convulsively, she said, in an almost inaudible voice, "I cannot, cannot go; have pity, Louis," she added, raising her tearful eyes to his.

"For an hour or two, and then you shall take care of baby."

"If—if—you would let me kiss her, I will lie down here, but I cannot leave her," she answered, almost choking.

"You may do that," he said, with a disagreeable sense of the fact that he had been unkind, to use no harsher term. And he lifted a weight from Natalie's heart, as he placed a shawl over her, saying, "try to sleep, dear; you know how much depends upon you," in sweet, modulated tones of thrilling tenderness, such as Louis knew well how to use—none better, when it suited him to do so.

It mattered not to little Izzie who tended her for many days; not so, however, when she began to mend, for now she would suffer none but mamma to touch her. She would scarcely bear to be put out of her arms. If Natalie attempted to lay her in the cradle, thinking she slept, instantly the tiny arms would be clasped round mamma's neck, and she would take her up again. No more could papa usurp mamma's rights; no coaxing or persuasion would induce her to allow him to take her. Only from mamma's hand would she take her medicine. On more than one occasion Natalie had to be aroused from the little sleep she allowed herself, to administer it. All this annoyed Louis beyond measure, but he did not again give way to his temper before the child, except on one occasion. He had, in the strongest terms, urged upon Natalie the importance of giving the medicine with regularity. The bottle was empty, and Natalie sent it down to be filled, but by some means it got mixed with the other medicines to be sent out, and was not returned to her. She suffered tortures for the want of it during his absence. When he returned, coming straight to baby as usual, he learned how it was, and found her worse for want of it, his indignation was extreme, and he heaped upon Natalie unjust and unmerited reproach, in harsh and bitter terms. His cruel words cut her to the heart, but her only answer was a gentle request that he would get it at once. Truly Isabel had not much to regret.

CHAPTER XXVI

"What do you think?" cried Rose, bursting into the school-room. "Everard is coming home."

"Oh, is he? I'm so glad," returned Alice.

"Yes; mamma had a letter to-day. He is better, and is coming home for change of air and mamma's good nursing. It was not Everard who wrote the letter, but the doctor, who is coming with him as far as Markham, and papa is to meet them there."

"When?" inquired Alice.

"To-morrow."

"And papa is away."

"Oh, he will be back to-night. Why, there is a carriage; I wonder who it is," she exclaimed, running to the window.

"How can you be so silly, Rose," interposed Isabel.

"Oh, it is Everard," she shouted, without heeding Isabel's remonstrance, "and that must be the Doctor. Oh, I'm so glad

Everard has come," and she danced about the room with glee.

"Rose, what a noisy child you are!" exclaimed Isabel, going to the window with the rest; but when she saw the Doctor, she became deadly pale, and had to lean against the window frame for support, but she had ample time to recover herself, as they were all too much occupied to observe her.

"How terribly ill he looks," said Rose.

"And how dreadfully weak," returned Alice. "I'm sure that gentleman was at Grace's party, only I forget his name."

"Oh, mamma and Grace are both out; who is to do the honors, won't you, Miss Leicester?"

"Oh, no."

"Do, there's a good creature," pleaded Rose. But Isabel was firm. "It will seem so queer," urged Rose.

"Alice, dear, *you* must go."

Oh no, indeed, I can't; please excuse me, Miss Leicester."

"Oh let *me* go," pleaded Rose, "I shall manage far better than Alice."

"You!" exclaimed Isabel, "nonsense! Alice has more thought, besides she has the advantage of two or three inches in height, at all events."

Alice remonstrated.

"Not another word, Alice, you have to go," said Isabel; and

Alice thought she had never seen Miss Leicester so peremptory.

Isabel was not afraid to trust Alice. Once fairly installed as hostess she would do very well, though shy at first.

"But he seems so very ill, and I shall not know what to do," said Alice.

"You must tell them they were not expected until to-morrow, to explain your mamma's absence; and I will order up some refreshments, and tell Norris to have your brother's room ready for him."

Poor Alice looked quite scared at the ordeal that was before her.

"Mind you manage nicely, Allie dear, and make your brother comfortable," said Isabel, kissing her. And Alice, with a great sigh, left the room.

Isabel would have been content to have done "the honors," as Rose termed it, had the Doctor been any other than Louis, but under the circumstances she was determined not to do so. Though firmly resolved to abide by this decision, she did not feel very comfortable, as she thought it not improbable that Everard would send for her. Indeed, he did tell Alice to bring her, but Alice, with her usual blunt manner, answered that Miss Leicester had refused to come, and had sent her. As Isabel had foreseen, Everard soon retired to rest after his journey, and she would have been nicely in for a long *tete-a-tete* with Louis, which she did not choose. As it was, she sent Rose to help her sister to entertain the Doctor until her mamma came home; and, taking Amy with her, Isabel retired to her own apartment, to prevent the possibility of meeting him.

The absentees returned early, and Mrs. Arlington came herself to request that Miss Leicester would endeavor to make the evening pass pleasantly to the gentlemen, as she and Grace had an engagement that evening, and as it was to be the ball of the season Grace did not wish to give it up.

"Pray, excuse me, Mrs. Arlington," Isabel began.

"Stay, Isabel, I know what you would say. The Doctor goes with us. Everard and his father will be alone, and I think you can find a song, a book, or something to amuse them."

"I will try," said Isabel, well content now that Louis was not to be of the party.

"One word more, Miss Leicester," said Mrs. Arlington, dismissing Amy. "I disapprove very much of the children being sent to entertain visitors, and I hope it will not occur again."

Isabel felt hurt, but merely replied, "under the circumstances it might be excused."

"No, Isabel, no; I cannot see any justifiable reason. It is more than two years since Dr. Taschereau was married, and if you have not got over that affair you ought to have done so, that is all I can say."

"I have, I have," exclaimed Isabel, warmly, "but still you could not expect me to meet him."

"I don't see why you should not; it would have been better to have done so than, by acting as you have, lead him to suppose that you have not overcome your former attachment."

"It is utterly impossible, for him to think that," returned Isabel hotly, "I told him differently long ago; no," she added indignantly, "I have not the slightest shadow of affection for him; but I cannot, will not, subject myself to his insufferable insolence. You don't know him, or you would not expect me to do so," and the hot tears welled up into her eyes.

"I cannot hear my son's friend aspersed, Miss Leicester, especially when he is my guest," said Mrs. Arlington, stiffly, "at the same time I don't, of course, mean to justify his former conduct towards you; and with regard to the children, do not let it occur again. You may make yourself happy about the doctor, as he returns by the early train in the morning, for he is anxious about his little girl, who is only now recovering from a serious illness."

On entering the drawing-room, Isabel found Everard on the sofa looking very pale and rather sad. "I am sorry to see you so ill," she said, "I came to give you a little music, but I'm afraid you will not be able to bear it."

"On the contrary I think it would do me good; but why would you not come this afternoon?"

"I am here now."

"But why not before? Was it not unkind?"

"It was not so intended."

"Will you not give me the reason?

"You must not ask me; believe that I had sufficient cause." The words were not such as he would have, but the manner was so winning that he could not choose but be satisfied. "I am here now, solely on your account, to amuse you as you like best. You must have been very ill," she said, regarding him kindly.

"Yes, I am awfully weak," he returned, "it seems so strange to me, I have usually been so strong."

"You will soon get strong here," replied Isabel, cheerfully.

"Not if you plague me as you did this afternoon," he said reproachfully.

"Don't be angry," she pleaded.

"Not angry, but hurt," he said.

"I couldn't help it," she answered, almost with a sob.

"It did seem a chilling reception, a strange coming home, so cold, so utterly without welcome, and I had longed so much to come.

"It was not my fault they were all out."

"Yes, they were all out, and you wouldn't come."

"You are angry," she was crying now, her face down on her hands.

"I am a brute," he said.

"Oh, no; but I am a naughty girl," and seating herself at the piano, she asked what he would have. She had not thought of the seeming neglect, she had not thought what he would feel at finding Alice the only one to receive him. She could not help it she told herself, perhaps so, but she had been selfish, very selfish; she was sorry, sorry that Everard should take it so hardly; but even so, did it occur again, she could not act differently. "What will you have," she asked.

"You know my favorites."

"Ah, that is right; I was just going to send for you," said Mr. Arlington, who now entered. "I see you know what will please him most; I don't know what we should do without you," he added warmly. "You don't know how good she has been to me, Everard, she is a good substitute for my gay party-going daughter, but for her I don't know what I should do now Emily is away." She is not good to me, thought Everard, and then a ray of hope sprung up, as he thought of her very kind manner, but no, had he not been led into thinking so before, but whenever he had touched ever so lightly on the old topic, he had been repelled.

Isabel felt sad to-night, and could only sing plaintive melodies, and then felt annoyed to think that she had failed to accomplish the purpose for which she came. But she was mistaken, these songs harmonized better with his present mood than more gay ones would have done.

Everard did not seem to gain strength. Isabel did her best to relieve the weariness of the long, long days: bringing the children into the library in the afternoon in order that he might share their amusement as she read aloud, and in various ways endeavored to lessen the monotony of the time. She would, perhaps, have acted more wisely had she not done so, for Isabel's was a very tender nature, and her gentle sympathy was very pleasant to Everard, but it only served to keep up the conflict between hope and fear, which was specially hurtful to him just now, when he needed perfect repose. But she thought Grace and her mother neglectful, and strove to make up for it. She often sent one of his young sisters to sit with him, but Rose was not allowed this privilege as often as the others, though on the whole she was best. Alice was too quiet, and Amy too apt to dwell on the perfections of her dear Miss Leicester, while Rose, her wild spirits subdued in the presence of her sick brother, but only sufficiently so to prevent her being oppressive, was just the cheerful companion that was good for him, her vigorous, healthy, happy-in-the-present style had a good effect. She was never at a loss for a topic for conversation, and her quick perception enabled her to detect at once when he grew tired, and then she would immediately employ herself in some quiet manner. She never sat contemplating him thoughtfully with eyes so like his own, as Alice too often did, as if she would read his very soul.

There did not appear to be much of "Mamma's good nursing" to which Rose had alluded. True it was a very gay season, and Mrs. Arlington's duties were very onerous. "You know, Everard," she said, "that Grace cannot go out alone, so that my time is so much occupied, that I fear I must appear very neglectful, but you understand it is not my wish to leave you so much," and Everard assented. But when he had a relapse, then she gave up society, and was all the attentive mother.

Louis was very skilful and had got him through a very severe illness, how severe they had not known till now. Mrs. Arlington sent the children into the country to be out of the way, and Isabel of course went with them.

CHAPTER XXVII

Baby is quite well and happy, in fact all trace of her illness has passed away; but Natalie is worn and weary with tending her pet and bearing with Louis's hasty temper; she is pale and wan, but ever sweet tempered. "Hark, baby, there's papa." Izzie ran to meet him. He raised her in his arms and caressed her, scarcely noticing his fond little wife, who would have been made happy by a kiss or kind word. Tired and weary, but with a heart ache which was harder to bear, Natalie lay on the sofa, she was nothing to him, that was clear.

"Love papa, baby, love papa," he said. Little Izzie threw her arms round his neck and kissed him, then struggled to get away, "What's the matter," he asked. "Love mamma, Izzie want's to love mamma." She ran to her mother and repeated the action. Natalie caught the child in her arms, kissing her passionately. "Izzie, my darling Izzie," she murmured, while large tears fell on the child's face. Taking up her pinefore Izzie gravely wiped her own face, and then tenderly endeavored to dry her mother's tears, whispering don't cry mamma, Izzie don't like to see mamma cry," and she nestled to her mothers side, stroking her hair and kissing her repeatedly. Nothing would have induced Izzie to leave her mother then, even had Louis attempted it, but he did not, he stood by the mantlepiece watching them, with an unpleasant sensation, that baby had no power to dry those tears. He remained there a long time, his head resting on his hand, while Natalie and baby fell asleep together. From time to time a deep, deep sigh would escape from Natalie, which was not pleasant for Louis to hear. Sarah came for baby, but he desired her to leave her there. After a while, he thought it was not best that she should be there, and went softly to the sofa and took her away. As he did so, he remarked for the first time—aye, for the first time—the worn unhappy expression of Natalie's sweet face, which did not leave it even in sleep, and stooping over her gave the kiss and kind words to his sleeping wife, which he had withheld when she might have been made happy by them. He carried the child to its nurse, then went to his surgery, busy among his drugs he could not but think of Natalie. How pale she looked, how fragile she had become, how languid and listless she seemed of late, he had noticed that, and with no pleasant feeling did he remember, that he had done so, only to chide her for being lazy. How blind he had been, he saw plainly enough that she needed change of air, she should have it, she should pay his uncle Macdermott a visit, and take Izzie with her, but what should he do without Izzie, he asked himself, but with surprising magnanimity, he refused to consider that question. He had been a little inattentive perhaps lately and owed her some amends, so Izzie should go with her. He knew very well that Natalie would never go without her, and, truth to tell, he had his misgivings as to how Izzie would behave without her mother, so, as he really thought it needful, it was as much necessity as kindness, that brought him to this decision.

Natalie submitted passively to all their arrangements, but, on the evening previous to their departure, when Louis was enjoying a cigar in the library, after superintending all the preparations for the next day's start, Natalie came fondly to his side, and laying her hand softly upon his shoulder, said in a voice that trembled with emotion, "I cannot go, do not ask me, Louis, I cannot, will not leave you," and her head sank on her hand, as she again murmured "do not ask me."

"Pooh, Natie, what nonsense," he answered, laughing.

"No Louis, I cant, you promised that you would come for a week, so I will wait until you can take the week, and then we will go together, but not now alone, O, not alone," and she sobbed out on his shoulder the pent up anguish of her heart. He drew her to him with more kindness than he had shown for a long time.

"You will not send me away," she whispered.

"Now, Nattie dear, be reasonable, you know you are not strong, and I want you to get your roses back, and a week would be too short a time to benefit you much, so in four weeks time I will come for two, that will do, won't it."

She shook her head, "I have a terrible dread of the journey, no Louis, I will not go, I will wait till you can come with me."

Louis was not one to submit to opposition, his brow grew dark and the fierce light was kindling in his eye. She should go, once for all he would not brook this resistance. After he had decided to let Izzie go to please her, and save all fuss, was this to be the end of it? no. "It is too late to say that now," he said, "a few weeks will soon pass, and this idle fear is childish."

"I should have spoken before, only I did so wish to please you if I could."

"No, Natalie," he said, sternly, "you do not care whether I am pleased or not, you think of nothing but your own foolish fancies."

"Don't be cross, Louis, it is because I love you so much that I want to stay, don't send me away, O Louis, don't."

"Now, Natalie, you are enough to provoke a saint," he said, angrily, "cross, indeed, no wonder if I am, don't let me hear another word about it, you go to-morrow."

Natalie saw that any more opposition would inevitably cause one of those fierce bursts of passion of which she ever stood in mortal dread; she glanced at his darkened countenance and was silent, but her heart was heavy.

"Come, we will take a turn on the lawn the moon is so bright," he said. They walked in the moonlight, those two, husband and wife not three years, but the happy brightness had faded out of her face, and the girl not twenty walked by his side with a weary step, as if life were almost a burden. She resolutely checked her tears, and silently paced the lawn, while her thoughts wandered back to the beautiful home in the south of France, where she first met the man who had proved so different a partner to what, in her love and trust, she had fondly imagined, and then she wished so fervently that she might even yet be to him all that she had hoped. But he did not want her with him, he would be glad when she was away, oh, he did not love her, or he would not thus cruelly insist upon her going. She had it in her heart even yet to throw herself into his arms and entreat him to let her stay, but she felt that it would be useless, besides she dare not offer further resistance to his will. She looked up into his face and knew she dare not.

His eyes were fixed upon her, "why Natalie," he said, laughing, "anyone would think I was an ogre to see your countenance." But it was not a pleasant laugh. Then the hardest thought that she ever had towards him, came to her mind, and she thought that he was acting very like one. Louis paused as they were about to enter the house saying, "You will not worry me any more, if you do it will be useless and only make me harsh," his manner was stern, determined and chilling in the extreme. Natalie shivered, "I will go," she replied in a choking voice, then flew up the stairs and alone in the dark gave vent to the grief that was breaking her heart. "Little fool," murmured Louis between his firmly closed teeth, "what a plague she is."

CHAPTER XXVIII

"O Isabel, it is nearly time for the train to pass, do let us go and watch for it," said Rose, and they went accordingly. "Here it comes, here it comes," she shouted, and the iron horse came on snorting and panting; nearer, nearer it approaches the bridge. 'Tis on the bridge. Crash—and in an instant, it is gone; the train with its living freight is a mass of broken ruins. The screams are appalling; the sight fearful in the extreme. The children ran back to the house trembling and awed, and huddled together in a frightened group. Among the first to be taken from the *debris* was a lady, and a little girl about two years old. Isabel offered her own room for the use of the sufferers, and some men carried them to the cottage, where kind nurse Bruce did all in her power until the doctor should arrive. Isabel took the beautiful child, who a few moments before was all life and animation, and laid it upon Bruce's bed; the poor little thing must have been killed instantly as there was no sign of suffering upon its face, but a large bruise on its temple. The doctor feared that the lady had received fatal injuries; all through the night she continued insensible, and the morning brought no change. Who she was they could not tell, but as Isabel sat watching her through the long night, she felt that she had seen her before, but where she could not recall. Late in the afternoon consciousness returned, and with a feeble moan she opened her eyes. "Where am I," she asked, "Oh, where is my little

Clotilda Jennings

Izzie?" Isabel's only answer was a kiss. "Don't say it," she cried, grasping Isabel's hand convulsively, "O, not that, not that! but I see it is so—I see it in your face without you saying so." "O, my baby, my baby, my little Izzie!" she moaned, covering her face with her hands; and then she lay quite still, her lips moving as if in prayer. The doctor, who came in shortly after, called Isabel from the room. "Miss Leicester," he said, "she will not live many hours, we had better find out who she is and summon her friends by telegraph. We can do so by sending to W—; I tell you candidly that she is past all human aid. Poor thing, she need not grieve for her child, she will be with her soon." They returned to the room to gain the desired information. "Send for Dr. Taschereau, at H—," she replied to the doctor's question. Now Isabel knew where and when she had seen her. But it grieved her to see what a change there was in the bright sunny girl who had cast such a cloud over her path at the ball at Elm Grove.

"Am I dying?" Natalie asked anxiously.

"I dare not give you false hope," the doctor replied.

She covered her face with her hands for a few moments. "Do you think I can live till Louis comes—Dr. Taschereau you know."

"I hope so," he answered, evasively.

"Make the telegram very strong; O, very strong. Say that I am dying, but be sure you don't say that baby is—you know—I can't say it," she said in a choking voice. "He will come, O, surely he will come," she murmured to herself. The doctor left promising to send immediately. "You are Isabel Leicester," Natalie said as soon as they were alone. "I am sure you are, for I have seen your picture."

"That is my name," replied Isabel, smiling, while she wondered how much Natalie knew about her.

"You loved Louis once?" she asked.

"Yes."

"You love him still?"

"No; that is past."

A smile of satisfaction illumined Natalie's countenance for a moment, but quickly left it. "I was always sorry for you, Natalie," Isabel said kindly.

"Sorry for me, why should you be sorry for me?" she asked quickly, then pausing a moment she added, sadly, "I see you know how it is."

"Ah, I know too well, I hoped, I prayed it might be otherwise."

"He does not mean to be unkind," she said, "but it is a cruel thing to know that your husband does not love you When I first found out that he did not, it almost killed me. He insisted on calling our little girl Isabel, in spite of all I could say as to my dislike to the name; so I thought it was his mother's name, though he would not say. But when I found out that it was yours, I was very angry; O, you must forgive me, for I have had very hard thoughts towards you, and now I know that you did not deserve them. O, Isabel, you are too good; I could not nurse you so kindly, had I been in your place. Let me see my little Izzie," she pleaded. Isabel brought the child to its mother; it looked sweetly calm in its marble beauty. "Bury us both together in one coffin," she said, while her tears fell fast upon its icy face. Natalie complained of great pain, nothing that the doctor could do seemed to give her any relief, and she lay moaning through the night. About six o'clock in the morning there was a quick step on the stairs which did not escape the ear of the sufferer. "Oh, Louis, Louis come to me," she cried. In a moment he was at her side, and her arms clasped round his neck. "I knew you would come," she said, fondly, "I could not have died happily unless you had."

He pressed her closely to him, while the hot tears fell upon her face, for he was now suffering bitterly for all his neglect and unkindness to his gentle little wife.

"O Louis, I have always loved you so much, so very much!" she said, clinging more closely to him, and gazing into his face with an intensity painful to witness, then smiling sweetly, she closed her eyes and all was over. The others retired from the room, and Louis was left alone with his dead wife, and had yet to learn the fate of his child.

During the time that elapsed before the funeral, Isabel carefully avoided meeting him, and hoped that he had not noticed her on the morning of his arrival. But just as he was about to leave, after that had taken place, and she was congratulating herself for having managed so nicely, a message was brought her that Dr. Taschereau wished to see her before he went. Though annoyed, Isabel did not see how she could very well refuse, so complied with the best grace she could. She found him in the sitting room, looking very pale. "I could not leave, Miss Leicester," he said, "without thanking you for your kindness to my wife. I had no right to expect it."

"I merely did my duty, and do not require any thanks."

"I would ask one question," he continued, with a strong

effort to be calm. "Was my little girl dead when first taken up?"

"Quite dead," she answered.

"It is a bitter trial," he resumed, "I loved my child unutterably; the blow seems to have crushed me, I have no longer any interest in anything, I have nothing left, nothing!"

Isabel was silent, she was thinking of the time when she had nothing left but him, and he had deserted her. And now it was the child he grieved for and not his dear little wife. His treatment of her, had always appeared to Isabel as his greatest fault, and her indignation was aroused as she saw, or thought she saw, that he did not feel her loss as he ought to have done. "I cannot but think," she said, "that the blow was sent in mercy to her, in whose future there could only be pain, weariness and silent suffering, and had she alone been taken, I can see that you would soon have got over it."

"You have no idea of the agony and remorse I have endured or you would not be so severe; you think because you know that I did not love my wife as I should, that I do not feel her loss, but you are mistaken, her angel gentleness and patience seem forever to upbraid me for my neglect and unkindness." And unable any longer to control his feelings, he laid his head on the table, while heavy sobs convulsed his frame. His passions were strong, and it was something fearful to witness the violence of his anguish. Isabel could not see his deep grief unmoved, yet dared not attempt to comfort him. Oh how she had wronged him; how keenly he felt his loss. She would not leave him, and yet she did not wish to stay, and turned away to hide her emotion. When he grew more composed, he advanced towards her saying, "It is getting late, Miss Leicester, once more I thank you for all your kindness."

"Do not think any more of my cruel words." said Isabel, the tears streaming from her eyes.

"Then you do not withhold your sympathy, even from me," he returned, offering his hand.

"How can I," she replied, taking, though reluctantly, the offered hand. "I am very sorry for you."

"Good news, Isabel, good news!" cried Alice coming in shortly after with an open letter in her hand. "Everard is out of danger, and is recovering rapidly, so we can soon come home, Mamma says."

"That is indeed good news," replied Isabel, who was really anxious to get the children home, as the late events had cast a gloom over all. Little Amy had more than once asked if Everard would die like the poor lady, and all three had cried very bitterly about the pretty little girl that was killed.

In three weeks more they were back at Elm Grove.

Everard was on the terrace to welcome them. He seemed very glad to see them again, but his manner towards Isabel was changed, he was cordial and kind, but still there was a difference. There was something inexplicable, and shall we say that it pained her. Why did she on retiring to her own room, shed bitter, bitter tears? She could scarcely have told, had you asked her, but so it was.

Now that Everard had resolved to turn his thoughts from Isabel more resolutely than ever, as it was useless any longer to indulge the hope of one day possessing her, and had determined upon becoming a divinity student, and as soon as possible be ordained and go as a missionary to some distant land, and there amid new scenes and duties forget his dream of happiness. Isabel found that she was not indifferent regarding Everard, and often drew comparisons between her old love and the would-be missionary, much to the disparagement of the former, and thought that he was unnecessarily strict with regard to the forbidden subject. Confess now, Isabel, do you not fancy since your return, that he has discovered the alteration in your feelings and is paying you in your own coin? Believing this, and thinking also, that he has ceased to care for you, is there not a coolness gradually springing up between you? Oh, Isabel, why did you on the night before he returned to college, throw his favorite song into the fire, saying that you were tired of that old thing, and did not think that you would ever sing it again? Were you not watching him when he took one step forward as if to save it, then turned away, the color mounting to his cheek and the veins of his forehead swelling? Oh, Isabel would you not gladly, gladly have sung it all the time if he had only asked you in the old way? Ah, it will be a long, long time before he will ask you again. You did more than you intended when you burnt that song. When at his father's request you sang, did he not instantly leave the room? Yes; and confess, Isabel, that you could with difficulty conceal your vexation. Did you not long to sing it with all your heart, and bring him back again? Oh, what a farce to burn that music; and yet, when he did return, did you not show him more coolness than you had ever done before?

Clotilda Jennings

CHAPTER XXIX

A year has passed since the events recorded in the last chapter; things have gone on much the same, Everard trying to appear indifferent, while in reality he was not so, but succeeding so well that Isabel felt almost ashamed of her preference for him, and was, also, only too successful in concealing her true feelings. She is now paying Emily a visit, though it was seldom that she could be persuaded to accept any invitation. But in justice to her old friends, it must be said that they often endeavored to do so. Ever since she came to Elm Grove she had always received abundant invitations for the holidays; but, with the exception of the Morningtons, Isabel had never been able to overcome her pride sufficiently to visit, in her present position, those she had known when in such different circumstances.

Harry and Emily, after travelling about for some time, had settled in H—, not far from the college, and had insisted upon Everard spending a great deal of his time with them, as they had fitted up a nice little study for his especial use.

Emily was very anxious for the ordination, and had announced her intentions to hear him preach his first sermon, let it be when and where it might, in spite of his saying that he would go where he was quite unknown.

"Now, Everard, I'm going to have a party on the fifth," said Emily, "and I want you to bring some of the students, and I should like very much to have tall, handsome ones, and none of your little 'ugly mugs.' I want particularly that nice Mr. Elliott you introduced to me the other day."

"I do not choose my friends merely for their appearance, and Elliott is not one of the students," returned Everard.

"Never mind who he is, I want him to come."

"I will ask him if he is in town; but I can't come, I am altogether too busy."

"Nonsense, Everard, you only say that to vex me. I mean you to come, that's pos'. Isn't he provoking, Isabel?"

"Perhaps his business is as important as it was that Christmas," said Isabel, quietly.

Everard looked up quickly from his book, but Isabel was fully employed with her tatting.

"What do you know about my engagements at that time?" he asked.

"Oh, nothing; only, perhaps, you can as easily put aside your work as you did then."

"How do you know that it was so easy?" he inquired.

"Only from appearances."

"Appearances are often deceitful."

"Very."

Again the rapid glance of inquiry, but he could make nothing of her placid countenance; and the single word "very," it must have been his own imagination that gave significance to the very decided manner in which she had uttered it, or did she, indeed, see through his assumed indifference?

"You speak as though you had some experience," he said.

Isabel crimsoned, for she felt very guilty.

"Do you try to appear different to what you are in reality?" he inquired.

"Do you?"

"Why do you ask?" he said.

"Why do you?" she retorted.

"Isabel, Isabel! the carriage will be here in five minutes," interposed Emily, "make haste and put your things on."

The fifth came in due course, and Mr. Elliott with it. "Let me introduce to you a partner," said Emily, taking him up to Isabel.

"We have known each other too long to need an introduction, have we not, Isabel?" he said pleasantly. Then turning to Emily he added, "Thanks, Mrs. Mornington, for an unexpected pleasure."

Everard, who was near by, heard him call her by her Christian name, and saw the warm welcome accorded him, and the evident pleasure the meeting caused Isabel. He was furiously jealous, and walked away intensely disgusted.

"You are a stranger here, are you not?" asked Emily.

"Oh, quite."

"Then I leave you in Isabel's hands."

"Could not be in better," he said, smiling, and Charley Elliott's smile was a very pleasant one. Emily was enchanted, and went to sing his praises to Everard, much to his annoyance.

"Upon my word, Emily, if I were Harry I should be positively jealous."

"Oh, jealousy is not Harry's *forte*; he leaves that to Mr. Everard Arlington," she said saucily, with a low curtsey and a most provokingly wise expression.

"Emily!"

"Don't be a goose, Evie."

"Where have you been this long, long time, Isabel?" asked Elliott, "I have missed you so much."

"Have you, Charley? I'm glad to hear that some one has missed me. The happy past seems almost like a dream, it seems so far away."

"It was too bright to last; don't you think so, Isabel?"

"Perhaps so."

"Ah, those were days to remember, the excursions I had with you and Harley. But I, too, have had my troubles," he added, gravely.

"Who is exempt?" she returned. "But what of Harley, foolish Harley? Whatever possessed him to go to India? But," she added, with a sigh, "it would not have availed him much to have stayed, as it turned out."

"I don't know; I think he would have done more wisely to have remained."

"Why he went, I never could fathom."

"You never knew?"

"Never. He assured me that he had good and sufficient reason, and that papa thought so, too."

"I didn't think them good, or sufficient either, but he wouldn't take my advice. It was our only quarrel, and I believe I have scarcely forgiven him yet for going. It would, I am convinced, have been better for all if he had not done so," and the tears stood in the young lieutenant's eyes. Though brave as a lion, Charley Elliott had a kind and loving heart. There was a soft, warm light in the deep-blue eyes; no one could know Charley Elliott without loving him. Everard had no mean rival, if Charley was one. But he was not. He loved Isabel, it is true, with all the warmth of his ardent nature, but he loved her as he might a beautiful sister. He thought her worthy of Harley—his Harley—the pride of his boyhood, who in his eyes could do no wrong, until one day when he told him that he was going to India. Charley's grief was excessive, but his indignation arose when he learned the cause.

Harley Elliott was ten years his brother's senior. He was the favorite clerk in the firm of Leicester & Co. Had Isabel to be met anywhere, and her father was unable to go, Harley was invariably sent; he was constantly at the house for one thing or another. As Isabel grew up he was frequently called upon to escort her and her young friends to places of amusement. As might be supposed, he became deeply in love with her, until at last life was almost a burden, for Harley was sensitive and high-minded to a degree: as a poor clerk, he was too proud to woo the rich merchant's daughter. He determined, therefore, to try to amass wealth in another land, and, if successful, to return and endeavor to win her; if not, to remain forever away.

But Charley, a boy of sixteen, could not appreciate this course. "Stay and be brave-hearted, Harley," he said, "she will, she must, love you, and the Governor will not refuse." But all he could obtain from Harley was a promise that he would tell Mr. Leicester the true cause of his going. Charley had great hopes as to the success of this course, but Harley was not so sanguine, and Harley was right. Mr. Leicester quite approved of his going, and offered him letters of introduction to parties at Calcutta. True, he inquired if the attachment was mutual. But when Harley confessed that he had not sought to know, considering himself in honor bound not to do so in his present circumstances, he was well satisfied that it was so. He took care, also, to find out if Isabel really had a preference for Harley, lest by urging his departure he might make her unhappy. And it must be admitted that he was glad to see that she was heart whole as yet, for he wished her to make a more brilliant match. So he wished Harley success, and did all in his power to hasten his departure.

Poor Charley had missed his brother sadly. He would have accompanied him but for his mother, who was not strong, and certainly could not have borne the climate.

"But your troubles, Charley; you have not told me of them," said Isabel. "Is not Harley doing well?"

Clotilda Jennings

"Yes, now; but it was some time first. I am going to see him soon. But it was my mother's death to which I alluded just now."

"Oh, have you lost your mother? Poor Charley!"

"Don't talk of her, Isabel, I can't bear it," and Charley brushed away a tear.

Dance succeeded dance, and Isabel was still Charley's partner. "There are half-a-dozen gentlemen dying to be introduced to Miss Leicester, and you give them no chance, Mr. Elliott," said Emily.

"Very well, but remember, Isabel, that we are engaged for the after-supper galop."

"I'll not forget," she returned.

Now it so chanced that Everard had so often been Isabel's partner for that dance, that he began to consider it a matter of course, and was highly offended when, after keeping away all the evening, he approached her, saying, "This is our dance, is it not, Miss Leicester?" and she replied, "You are too late, Mr. Arlington," and whirled off with Charley Elliott.

"Why did you do that?" he asked, when Isabel was again seated.

"Was I to refuse a partner in case Mr. Arlington, after keeping away all the evening, should condescend to ask me? I think you expect too much."

"You knew I should come."

"How could I know?"

"I always do."

"And do you always keep away all the evening?"

He bit his lip. "Will you dance this?"

"I am engaged."

"The next."

"Impossible, my card is quite filled up."

"Never mind, you can strike out one of the names."

"Why should I do so? You had the best chance; you were here from the first, but from some whim determined not to put down your name, and looked glum whenever I passed you, and now you think that I will treat one of these young men so unhandsomely. No, Mr. Arlington, I will not."

"You chide me for not coming sooner. I thought you so well amused that I was not needed."

"Needed, no; but still you have not been commonly civil to-night."

"You are very unforgiving."

"No, but I will not encourage your whims; you chose to sulk, it was no fault of mine."

"As you will."

"I think this dancing awfully stupid," he said to Emily, as Isabel went off with her partner, "I shall be glad when it is over."

"Of course," she replied, with a most provoking laugh.

"Parsons don't usually care for dancing," added Harry, in a tone equally irritating.

But for Charley Elliott the evening would have been dull enough to Isabel. She would far rather have had Everard for a partner than any of those whose names were on her programme, but she believed that he had purposely avoided her all the earlier part of the evening: besides, Everard's manner towards her of late had become quite an enigma—now cold, almost haughty, then again soft, even tender, then indifferent—and Isabel resented its variableness. She was the more annoyed, as she knew that Emily was not quite in the dark.

"I think Mr. Elliott is a very nice young man, don't you, Isabel?" said Emily at breakfast next morning.

"Very," replied Isabel, coloring warmly as she caught Everard's penetrating glance.

"A done thing, I see," laughed Harry.

"How can you be so absurd, Harry?"

Are you fond of sea voyages?" he continued.

"I think them delightful."

"Capital. Did you know that he was going to India?"

"Yes."

"You did? Well, really."

"Oh, Harry, be quiet."

"I thought you two seemed awfully good friends. Did you know him before last night?"

"Certainly."

"I am sure you don't agree with Everard that the party was a dreadfully slow affair?"

"Oh, no; it was very pleasant."

"I was very sure that Miss Leicester did not find it dull," said Everard coldly, almost scornfully.

"Goosey, goosey!" said Emily, later in the day, as she came upon Everard in the music-room.

"Why do you go on in this provoking way, Emily?" he said, angrily.

"Because I have no patience with this stupid jealousy. If you care for her, why not try to win her in a straightforward manner; if not, why be vexed that another should?"

"Why do you strive to undo that which has cost me so much? She is nothing to me; I have determined that she shall be nothing."

"Then why so jealous?"

"I cannot help it; you know that I cannot."

"But why force yourself to give her up?"

"Why, indeed," he echoed, "is it not worse than useless to

cherish an attachment for one who is so perfectly indifferent?"

"I do not believe that she is as indifferent and inaccessible as you imagine."

"Why do you tempt me, Emily?" he returned, almost fiercely. "Let me be; the ordination will be very shortly, and I am sure of an appointment directly after."

"Ah, goosey, goosey! 'Faint heart,' you know," she said, and left him—more angry with his favorite sister than he had ever been before.

CHAPTER XXX

"Isabel, you said something about going home this week; now I have settled that for you. I wrote to mamma, saying that you were going to stay until after the ordination, and then we would all return together."

"I declare those children will get quite unmanageable with such long holidays. When will the ordination be?"

"The beginning of next month."

"Dreadful! I do not think that Mrs. Arlington will consent."

"Oh, yes, she will. What a state Everard is getting into about that ordination!" she continued, "and I am nearly as bad. I suppose we shall all go to see it."

"I shall not," said Isabel.

"Why not?" asked Emily.

"I had rather not."

"What a strange girl you are! I wouldn't miss it for the world. He will be so vexed, too."

Clotilda Jennings

"Why should he?"

"Of course he will."

Isabel protested that she would not go; but for all that, when the time came, she could not resist the desire to be present, even at the risk of being thought changeable. She went, after the rest, and from her corner saw the whole. From where she sat she had a full view of his face—grave, earnest, calm, evidently feeling how much was implied in the ordination vows. As she returned before the others, they were quite unaware that she had been there, and she, little hypocrite, listened gravely to all Emily's descriptions.

In the evening Isabel walked on the lawn in the pale moon's silvery beams, musing of all that had taken place that day, and thinking how very happy Everard must feel to-night. Suddenly that gentleman accosted her: "Why did you refuse to be present at the ordination to-day?" he asked. Isabel was silent. "How is it," he continued, "that while others were so anxious, you manifested no interest at all? It is, to say the least, unkind."

"You may be sure that I wish you all prosperity in your new vocation," she said. "I would have said so before, had I thought you wished or expected it."

"I did not expect," he said, almost angrily, "such a calm expression of a cold regard; I wished and expected kindly sympathy, if nothing more."

"As you think I should say more, accept my sincere wishes for your happiness; and believe me when I say that the lot which you have chosen is, in my estimation, the highest to which man can aspire, and may your labors be blessed with abundant success."

"Your kind wishes, though so reluctantly expressed, are not least valued," he returned, warmly. "But, Isabel, you say that you wish my happiness. My happiness, as I told you long ago, rests with you. Here I can refer to the old subject without breaking my promise, and I cannot leave for my distant mission without making one more appeal. Listen to me patiently for a few minutes. You seemed to adhere so strictly to what you said, that I considered it my duty to give you up; but it was a duty that, with all my endeavors, I was unable to perform. I sought relief in study—hard, excessive study—almost night and day. You know how that ended. My mother left me much to you, and your kindness only made matters worse. Afterwards, when you were away, I determined on the course I am now pursuing, and I persuaded myself that my heart was in the work, and so it is, but it is not yours the less. What I endure is almost insupportable—it is too hard. Often I have been obliged to appear cold and variable to conceal my real feelings, and you have despised me for it. I have seen it, Isabel. To-night I determined to seek you, and plead my cause once more; and though you have received me with indifference, even coldly, I still hope that beneath this reserve there may be some warmer feeling. "Tell me dearest," he continued, "will you not love me? Oh, Isabel, must I go alone?" She was silent. Then for an instant her eyes met his, and the love and happiness in that one glance fully satisfied him, and he clasped her passionately in his arms. "You loved me all the time, Isabel," he whispered, "only from a mistaken sense of your duty you refused me when I first spoke of my love."

"Oh, no, I did not love you then; I esteemed you very much, but I was engaged to another." Then she told what is already known to the reader.

"And his name?" he asked.

"Louis Taschereau."

"Tell me: did the thought that I loved you tend to soften the blow, when you found how unworthy he was?"

Isabel was very truthful; she could not deceive him, even though those beautiful eyes were fixed upon her in earnest expectation. As we have said, she was very truthful, so answered, "I cannot flatter you so much, Everard; it afforded me no comfort whatever. Indeed I never thought of it, except when some kind attention on your part reminded me of the fact, and then the thought only caused me pain."

He looked disappointed. "No," she added, "it was not until long after, that your worth and uniform kindness won my heart."

They lingered on the lawn until the chill night air warned them not to remain there any longer. Entering the music-room by the window, they found Emily waiting for them. "Oh, here you are at last; Harry had to go out, and I've been all alone this half hour." Then, starting up, she seized a hand of each, exclaiming "You need not tell me, I see how it is; I am so glad, so very glad."

"I saw you at the ordination this morning," said Charley Elliott, who came in during the evening, addressing Isabel, "only you were in such a fearful hurry to get away that I did not get a chance to speak."

"Then you must have very good eyes, Mr. Elliott, as Isabel was not there," cried Emily, laughing.

"I beg your pardon," he returned.

"I was there," said Isabel quietly, though she colored hotly.

"You were?" exclaimed Everard, evidently well satisfied.

"I declare you—are—a queer girl," said Emily, opening her blue eyes very wide, "I'm afraid you have not the bump of firmness."

"I knew you would think me changeable, but after you had all gone I began to think I should like to see it, so I followed. But I certainly did not see you, Charley."

"On, no, I was very sure that you saw no one but the candidates," returned Charley, laughing. "Indeed you looked so solemn and earnest, one would almost suppose that you were one of them."

"Is it true," asked Harry, on his return, "that you have agreed to start for Madagascar next month?"

"Quite true," returned Everard, coolly.

"I protest against it," said Harry. "And so do I," added Emily; while Charley shrugged his shoulders, and Isabel laughed.

Emily was terribly anxious for Charley to depart, as she longed to tell Harry the news; which news, when Emily told it, Harry received with unmistakable satisfaction, saying he couldn't see why Everard should not settle down comfortably near home, instead of going to such an out-of-the-way place.

The following week they all started for Elm Grove, and when, on their arrival Mrs. Arlington took both her hands and kissed her affectionately, Isabel knew that the news of their engagement had preceded them. They had a delightful evening, Mrs. Arlington being in a most gracious humor. Mr. Arlington shook Isabel so heartily by the hand that it ached for hours afterward. Emily was in the most exuberant spirits;

Everard's happiness, from its very depth, was of a more quiet nature; while Harry was as merry and joyous as his wife; and Isabel, in her own sweet way, had a kind look and word for all.

On entering the school-room, next morning, Isabel found little Amy sitting upon the floor, her head buried in the sofa cushion, sobbing as if her heart would break, her little form quivering with the violence of her emotion.

"What is the matter, Amy dear?" asked Isabel, taking the trembling child in her arms. But Amy could not speak; she only clung to Isabel, and sobbed more bitterly than before. Isabel sat down with Amy on her knee, stroking the shining hair until the child should be more composed. After a time, when the violence of her grief had a little abated, Isabel kissed her and inquired the cause of her tears.

"Rose says that you are going to Madagascar with Everard, and perhaps I shall never see you any more," she managed to blurt out amid her sobs. "You ought not to go, for I am sure I love you more than he does. I told him so this morning, but he only laughed and said I didn't; but I do, and I think it is very unkind of him to take you away. We know lots of young ladies; I'm sure he might marry some one else, and not take my darling Isabel to nasty Madagascar. Oh, Isabel, you must not go. Oh, please! please!" she said, coaxingly. "Oh, won't you please tell him that you have changed your mind, and would rather stay with us?"

"Oh, but you know I promised, Amy."

"But you shan't go; tell him you won't; there's a dear, kind pet," and she threw her arms round Isabel's neck.

"But don't you think that it is very selfish of little Amy to wish that her brother should go alone to that far country, when she will have papa, mamma, and sisters?"

"Oh! I wish you didn't love him one bit, and then you would stay with us."

"Hush! Amy dear, you mustn't talk so."

"But I can't help wishing it, and I told Everard so, and that I hoped you would change your mind. Then he said that it was very wicked of me to wish that; and he put me off his knee so quick, and walked out of the room looking so angry—no, not angry, exactly, but as if he thought, perhaps, you might."

"But, Amy, if you loved any one very much, would you like it if that person didn't love you one bit?"

"No," said Amy, thoughtfully.

"Then is it doing as you would be done by to wish such unkind and selfish things?"

"I did not think of that," replied Amy, resting her head on Isabel's shoulder, "but it seems as if you did not love me, to go away to Madagascar," she added, sadly.

"Oh, Amy dear, I love you very much," said Isabel, the tears gathering in her eyes, "and it grieves me to part from you."

"And then we shall have another horrid governess, like Miss Manning, and the days will all be long and miserable, like the long, long, weary day that Emily used to sing about. And what will become of all our nice Sundays?"

"Poor little Amy!" said Isabel, parting back the shining curls from the sorrowful little face, and looking into the violet eyes that were fixed upon her so earnestly. "You must not think that I would leave you without first trying to fill my place with one who would love you and try to make you happy. Now, if you will stop crying, I will tell you about the young lady who, I hope, will be your governess. She is a very dear friend of mine, and I trust you will all be very kind to her, and love her very much. Her name is Gertrude Hartley." Alice and Rose now entered the school-room, and gave a very warm welcome to Isabel. "Please go on about Gertrude Hartley," pleaded Amy. Then Isabel told them how Gertrude had gone as a governess to a family who lived far back in the country, miles away from any church, and how, by her endeavors, a small but pretty one had been erected, where service was held once a month. But Gertrude had grown tired of the country, and was anxious to obtain another situation. "She will come to see you next week, and I am sure you will like her. And you know you can often talk about me, for she knows me very well. I shall write you nice long letters about that strange country, and I shall often think of my dear little sisters, for you will be my sisters then, you know."

"I did not think of that," said Amy, smiling.

"Oh, Isabel, I'm so sorry that you are going away. Don't you think you could persuade Everard to give up being a missionary? I'm certain he could have Attwood Church if he liked, because Dr. Herbert once asked him if he would like it. Please do, because it would be so nice."

"What! and leave those heathen people still in ignorance of God? My little Rose does not think what she is wishing that Everard would give up. No, I could not wish him to do so, much less persuade him."

"But he might get some one else to go," replied Rose.

"No, Rose, we must each perform our own duties."

"You mean that it would be like putting your hand to the plow and looking back?"

"Exactly so," replied Isabel.

"I did not think of it in that way, so you must not be angry with me."

"I was not angry, dear, only I wanted to show you that your wish was a wrong one. What does Alice think about it?"

"I think," replied Alice, "that he ought to go, and I am very glad that you are going with him, for you are so nice and so good that I am sure the little heathen children will listen to what you say, because you have such a nice way of telling things. Of course I am very sorry to lose you, but I mean to think of the good your going will be for other people, and how nice it is for Everard, and then I shall not care about it so much."

"It gives me great pleasure to hear you say this, and I think that Alie can no longer be called selfish. Believe me, dear children, that the surest way to forget our own troubles is to find pleasure in the benefit and happiness of others."

Everard Arlington was about to enter by the window, but paused a moment to contemplate the group before him. On a large ottoman sat Isabel, with Amy on her knee, one arm encircling Alice, who was standing thoughtfully by her side, her head resting on Isabel's shoulder, while behind was Rose, half smiles, half tears.

"Oh, Everard!" cried Amy, "I won't say again that I hope Isabel will not go with you. But she says that it is not naughty to be sorry. You are not angry with me now?" she inquired, looking wistfully into his face.

"No, my little Amy," he replied, smoothing the glossy curls, as he stooped as if to kiss her, but he didn't kiss Amy.

CHAPTER XXXI

Mrs. Arlington was not one to do things by halves, so that when she welcomed Isabel, on her return, it was no longer as "the governess," but as her future daughter-in-law—as the bride-elect of her darling son—indeed as one of them, the Arlingtons. She was glad, as he was so determined upon being a missionary, that he was to marry before he went, but she would rather—far rather—that he should have chosen any other than "the governess," though she had nothing against Isabel—nothing. Still it was a trial to the haughty mother that her only son—the hope and pride of the family—should marry a governess. She knew that many would say she had been imprudent in having so young and pretty a governess, knowing how fond Everard was of the society of his young sisters. And, indeed, she did feel she had been wrong when she got Everard's letter announcing the engagement, and it was some little time before she could be at all satisfied with the matter. Grace was excessively annoyed, and, by her anger, tended greatly to stimulate her mother's displeasure, saying that it was quite a disgrace to the family, and that she would never receive Isabel as a sister. Fortunately her consent was never likely to be asked, as her easy-going brother, the pet of the house, had a pretty determined will, and her opinion would certainly not influence him in the matter. Indeed, now that he had Isabel's consent, he would have married her even though opposed by

Clotilda Jennings

any number of relations; and it was with no thought of obtaining their ideas on the subject that he had written, but simply to inform them of the fact, little suspecting the commotion it would cause at Elm Grove.

However, the course he pursued had the effect of reconciling his mother to the match, and it was well that it was so, or Isabel would have met with a sorry reception on her arrival.

Very quickly after the letter we have mentioned, came another, such as only Everard could write—written out of a full heart, telling of his happiness, and also of his former despair, long probation, and weary waiting; how his love for Isabel had dated from that Sunday evening when he first saw her in the school-room with the children; and expressing the hope that his mother would give Isabel a place in her heart equal to that of her own children.

Tears of sympathy and love fell from the mother's eyes as she read, and a happy smile played around her mouth as she refolded the letter which would be read again and again. Henceforth she was won. So, then, when Lady Ashton, who had now returned from England, came to condole with dear Mrs. Arlington upon the ill luck that had befallen the family, she found that lady quite satisfied, to her profound astonishment. However, she gave a willing ear and ready sympathy to Grace, who was quite disgusted at her mother's contentment, and returned with Lady Ashton to the Park, saying, that she was far too angry to meet them at present; and there she remained for weeks nursing her wrath against her only brother, who would so shortly leave for a distant land, not heeding the possibility, nay probability, that he might never return. Who could foresee the dangers that might be in store for him? Read the dangers and miseries to which the missionaries sent to foreign and heathen lands are only too often subjected—dangers on sea and land, and fearful cruelties at the hands of wild and savage creatures, more ferocious sometimes in their implacable fury than the beasts of prey. But even overlooking these more dreadful calamities, there is the climate, so trying to the natives of cooler countries. Nor was she just to Isabel. She would only see a beautiful, designing girl, who had succeeded in catching her brother. She was angry with Isabel, with Everard, with her mother, and, lastly, with herself, to think that she, too, had been for a short time deluded like the rest. She felt now that she positively hated Isabel.

Lady Ashton did her best to fan the flame of resentment. What wonder, then, that under that lady's able management it grew day by day, until Grace really believed her silly anger to be just indignation at her brother's blind infatuation. Ah, foolish Grace!

To Emily's great satisfaction, Everard preached his first sermon in the church they usually attended, and was very calm and self-possessed considering the eight eager faces in the family pew, his heightened color being the only evidence that this was the first time he had addressed a congregation from the pulpit. It happened, strangely enough, that a collection for the Missionary Society was to be taken up on this occasion, and the young deacon delivered an exceedingly eloquent discourse advocating the cause of missions, with a warmth and earnestness that carried his hearers along with him, and showed that his heart was in the work. No one who heard him could doubt his future success in the cause.

Then what a happy group waited for him after service, and what approving smiles beamed upon him from loved faces when he came!

"Oh, Everard! I should never go to sleep at sermon time if you always preached," cried little Amy. "It was so nice," added Rose, warmly; while the proud father wrung his son's hand in silence more eloquent than words.

Then Everard disappointed a crowd of admiring friends by disappearing through a side gate and going home across the fields, even waving back his young sisters, who would have followed him. "I could not stand it," he said, on reaching home half an hour after the others, though his way had been much shorter, he having spent the interim in self-communion beneath the shade of a friendly oak. Oh! that was a happy Sunday at Elm Grove; but, like all earthly happiness, it had one cloud—Grace's strange and unkind conduct.

CHAPTER XXXII

"Please, Miss Leicester, a gentleman wishes to see you," said Susan, putting her rosy face in at the school-room door, as Isabel was giving the children their last lesson.

"To see *me*, Susan?" exclaimed Isabel.

"Yes, Miss, he asked for you, but he would not give his name."

"Very well, Susan. Who can it be?" she asked, turning to Alice.

"I'm sure *I* don't know," answered Alice, laughing, "you had better go and see."

On entering the drawing-room, Isabel saw to her astonishment that it was Louis Taschereau. "This is indeed a surprise," she said, extending her hand, for in her present happiness she could not be ungracious or unkind.

Encouraged by her cordial greeting, Louis began: "I thought of writing, but determined on seeking an interview, as a letter could but inadequately convey what I wished to say. I have suffered much, as you are aware, and my troubles have made me a very different man; but a gleam of light seems

Clotilda Jennings

once more to shine on my path, and I hope yet to repair the error of my life. Can you—will you—overlook and forgive the past, and be again to me all that you once were? I know that I do not deserve it, but I will try to atone for the past if, dear Isabel, you will be my wife."

"Stay, Dr. Taschereau!" interposed Isabel, "I am just about to marry a clergyman who is going abroad."

Had a cannon-ball fallen at his feet, Louis could scarcely have been more dumbfounded than he was at this intelligence. He became deadly pale, and she thought he would faint.

"You are ill, Dr. Taschereau. Let me ring for some wine."

"Don't ring, I don't want any. Is this true?" he continued, "are you really going to marry another?"

"I am, and I do not see why you should be surprised."

"Why do you make me love you so? Why must your image intrude itself into every plan, and all be done as you would approve, if, after all, you are to marry another? You would not wonder at the effect of what you have told me, if you knew how the hope that you would forgive me and yet be mine, has been my only comfort a long, dreary time."

"You have no right to speak in this way, Dr. Taschereau; it was I who had cause of complaint, not you. But I am very sorry that you should feel so; very sorry that you should have suffered yourself to imagine for a moment that we could ever be again to each other what we once were. And do not think that my present engagement is the cause of my saying this; for never, never, under any circumstances, could I have been your wife after what has passed. I say not this in anger or ill-will for the past, I do not regret it—I feel it was best."

"Will you not tell me the name of the fortunate clergyman?" he asked.

"Certainly, if you wish it; it is no secret. It is Everard Arlington."

"Everard Arlington!" he exclaimed in unfeigned astonishment. "It was the knowledge of his hopeless attachment that made me hope—almost make sure—that you had not entirely ceased to love me, and might yet be mine; the more despairing he became, the higher my hopes rose."

"How could you, how dared you, indulge such thoughts after what I said in the woods at D—?" exclaimed Isabel, indignantly. "If Everard had so long to believe that his attachment was unavailing, it was because Isabel Leicester would not give her hand unless her heart went with it; because I respected his affection too much to trifle with it, and not at all on your account. Believe me, that from the time I first learned that you were married, every thought of you was rigidly repelled, and it was arrant presumption in you to suppose anything else," she continued, proudly, the angry tears suffusing her eyes.

The conference was here ended, to Isabel's great relief, by the entrance of Everard, who looked inquiringly at each.

"How are you, old fellow?" he said (for Isabel's proud anger fled at his approach), "what brought you here so unexpectedly?"

"Oh, a little private affair," he replied, looking rather uncomfortable; but there was that in Louis's eye, as he said this, that made Isabel distrust him; something that made her determined to put it out of his power to misrepresent and make mischief. True, he had said how changed he was, and spoken of the reformation his trials had made. Certainly he had been more calm under disappointment than had been his wont. But still she doubted him. She had seen that look before, and knew that it was the same false Louis, not so changed as he imagined. The dark side was only lying dormant; she could read his malicious enjoyment in that cruel smile, and knew its meaning well. Meeting his glance with one of proud defiance and quiet determination, which said, as plainly as words, "I will thwart your fine plans, Mr. Louis," she said:

"You are aware that I was formerly engaged to Dr. Taschereau. His business here to-day was to endeavor to renew that engagement. I need not say how very strange and absurd this appears, as you are acquainted with the circumstances under which the former engagement terminated."

"Yes, that was the 'little private affair,' but I find that you have already won the prize; allow me to congratulate you."

Louis said this in a frank, pleasant manner, appearing to take his own disappointment with so much good nature, at the same time blending a certain degree of sadness in his tone as quite to deceive Everard and win his sympathy. But the thundering black look which he cast at Isabel fully convinced her that she was right.

"You will dine with us, of course," said Everard, cordially.

"I shall do so with pleasure," returned Louis.

Isabel bit her lip. "Just to see how much he can annoy me," she thought. But if this was his object he must have been disappointed, so totally unconscious of his presence did

Isabel appear, and when he addressed her personally her manner was colder than even Everard thought necessary.

The heat of the rooms became very oppressive during the evening, and Isabel stepped out on the lawn to enjoy the refreshing breeze, but was soon surprized to find that Louis had followed her.

"Let us at least be friends," he said. "You will remember that it was not in anger we last parted."

But Isabel was silent.

"You doubt me," he continued. "I do not blame you, but you are harsh, Miss Leicester."

"Not harsh, but just," returned Isabel. "Friends we can never be; enemies I trust we never were."

"You draw fine distinctions. May I ask what place in your estimation I am permitted to occupy?" said Louis, sarcastically.

"No place whatever, Dr. Taschereau; I must ever regard you with indifference," returned Isabel, coldly.

"Be it so," he replied, angrily. "You have obstinately refused all offers of reconciliation, and must therefore take the consequences."

"The consequences? You speak strangely, Dr. Taschereau."

I repeat: the consequences. I determined long since that you should never marry another, and my sentiments on that subject have not changed. No; I vow you shall not!" he added, with the old vindictive expression.

"How dare you hold such language to me, sir?" cried Isabel, indignantly.

Without answering, he drew a pistol from his pocket and would have shot her, but, changing his purpose, he turned upon Everard, who was approaching. With a cry of horror, Isabel threw herself between them, and prevented Louis from taking as good an aim as he might otherwise have done; for though the ball, in passing, grazed her shoulder, it passed Everard harmlessly and lodged in the acacia tree. With parted lips, but without the power of speech, she clung to Everard in an agony of terror for a moment, and then lay motionless in his arms. In terrible apprehension he carried the senseless girl into the house, fearing that she was seriously hurt, as the blood had saturated a large portion of her dress, which was of very thin texture. Of course the consternation into which the family was thrown by the shot, followed by the entrance of Everard with Isabel in this alarming condition, was tremendous. But happily Isabel was more terrified than hurt, Dr. Heathfield pronouncing the wound of no consequence (to Everard's intense disgust), telling her to take a glass of wine and go to bed, and she would be none the worse for her fright in the morning—in fact treated the whole thing quite lightly, and laughed at Isabel for her pale cheeks, saying that such an alabaster complexion was not at all becoming. He promised to send her something to prevent the wine making her sleep too soundly, meaning a composing draught to enable her to sleep, as he saw very little chance of her doing so without. Everard volunteered to go with him for it. On their way, Dr. Heathfield remarked that he was afraid Everard thought him very rude and unfeeling. Everard, who had been very silent, replied that he did.

"Then do not think so any longer," said the Doctor, laying his hand on his companion's shoulder. "I saw how scared she was, and treated the case accordingly. You are both great favorites of mine, so I hope you will not be offended. Do you know what became of the scoundrel?"

"He made for parts unknown immediately after he fired," replied Everard, sternly, while the heavy breathing showed how much it cost him to speak calmly. "It is quite a Providence that one of us is not dead at this moment, as he is a splendid marksman. I don't know which of the two the shot was intended for; if for me, she must have thrown herself between us."

"She is just the girl to do it," cried the Doctor, grasping him warmly by the hand. "I have always had a very high opinion of her."

"I should think so," said Everard, with a quiet smile of satisfaction.

Fortunately Isabel had no idea that Everard had gone with the Doctor, or she would have been terribly anxious, for fear Louis should still be near. But guilt makes cowards of all, so Louis was now in a fearful state of mind: for he was passionate, hasty, violent and selfish, but not really bad-hearted, and jealous anger and hatred had so gained the mastery over him that he had been impelled to do that at which, in cooler moments, he would have shuddered. So now he was enduring agony, fearing lest his mad attempt at murder had been successful, yet not daring to inquire. Ah, Louis! you are now, as ever, your own worst enemy."

Clotilda Jennings

CHAPTER XXXIII

"What makes you look so sad Everard; Isabel was not much hurt; not hurt at all I may say."

"I was not thinking of her just now Emmy," he answered smiling, but the smile passed away, and left his face very sad indeed.

"What is it Evvie," she asked in the old coaxing way, seating herself beside him on the seat round the old Elm tree.

"I was thinking of Grace," he replied "you can't think how her keeping away pains me."

"I wouldn't think of it, if I were you, it is very mean and ill-natured of her, but she will get over her huff after a while."

"That would be all very well, if I were going to remain here, but you know how soon I go and—"

"Oh Everard," (Emmy could not contemplate this event with composure) "Oh Everard, I can't bear you to go, and she threw her arms round his neck, weeping passionately.

His sisters were not much given to tears, this one in particular, the brightest of them all, so that this genuine bust of grief was the more perplexing.

He was endeavouring in vain to soothe her, when little Emmy came upon the scene, and seeing her mamma in trouble, she set up a terrific howling, and running at Everard, she seized his coat to steady herself and commenced to kick him with all the force she could muster, exclaiming "naughty, naughty, to make my mamma cry."

This warlike attack upon her brother set Emily laughing, while he feigned to be desperately hurt by the tiny feet at which the round blue eyes grew wonderfully well satisfied. Isabel now joined them alarmed by the cries of her little playmate. Emmy looking very brave scrambled upon mamma's knee, from whence she darted very defiant glances at her uncle.

"I think I will go to Ashton Park" said Everard.

"Do you think that it will do any good" asked Emily.

"I hope so, Grace is not bad hearted, only vexed, besides, I should wish to leave on good terms with the old lady."

"I have no doubt that she pities you immensely." Everard laughed "I will go now" he said, "and we hope you may be successful" returned both warmly.

"Good evening Lady Ashton" said Everard when he arrived at the Park; entering the drawing-room from the lawn.

"Oh is that you, you poor unfortunate boy," returned her ladyship compassionately.

"Pray spare your pity, for some more deserving individual," answered Everard laughing, "I think myself the most fortunate of mortals."

"Don't come to me with your nonsense, you are very silly, and have behaved in a most dishonorable manner towards your family."

"Will you be kind enough to state in what way," replied Everard colouring, "I confess I can't see it."

"Why, in offering to that governess girl."

"You are severe."

"Oh I haven't patience with you; my sympathy is all with poor Grace, who feels quite disgraced by it."

"She cannot think so, seriously, or if she does, she ought to be ashamed.

"Hoighty, toighty, how we are coming the parson to-night."

"Pshaw," exclaimed Everard impatiently.

"I think she is justly angry and aggrieved. Of course in receiving so young and pretty a girl, as governess for your sisters, (for I allow that she is pretty.) "Oh you do," said Everard sarcastically. "Your mother" continued Lady Ashton "relied upon your honorable feelings, and good sense, but you have abused her confidence in a most cruel manner."

The swelling veins, and heavy breathing showed how annoyed he was, and he answered warmly, "I deny having done anything wrong or dishonorable, I presume that I have a perfect right to choose for myself."

"To a certain extent I grant, but you owe something to the

feelings of your family."

"They have no cause of complaint, Isabel is quite their equal if not superior."

"In your estimation," said Lady Ashton contemptuously.

"I don't care to discuss the subject" returned Everard haughtily.

"Reverse the matter, how would you like it, if Grace was going to marry a tutor."

"If he was a worthy person, and Grace was satisfied, I certainly should not object."

"I doubt it," cried Lady Ashton angrily. Then she commenced aspersing Isabel in every way, and Everard hotly defended her. "Nasty, artful, designing girl, you will live to repent your folly yet," she said. Then Everard got in a terrible passion newly ordained though he was. But Lady Ashton was a woman, and Everard Arlington never forgot when he was in the presence of ladies, so though they most decidedly quarrelled, Everard saying some pretty severe things, he managed to keep the cooler of the two, Lady Ashton being as spiteful as only Lady Ashton could be. So instead of conciliating Grace he had only made matters worse; as he supposed; but Lady Ashton really loved her god-son, and in her heart admired him for his spirit.

Everard's anger once roused was not easily appeased, so that after he left Ashton Park, he took a ten mile walk in the moonlight before he was sufficiently calm to venture home. "What is the matter" asked his mother when he did.

"I have been in a tremendous passion, and am not quite

cooled down yet" he answered, "good night."

The upshot of all this was, that on coming home one afternoon, Everard found Lady Ashton, and Grace waiting for him. "Let bygones, be bygones," said the former taking his hand, while Grace offered hers with a dignified condescension that was truly amusing, Everard was only too glad to have a cessation of hostilities, and responded cordially to the overtures of peace.

Then Lady Ashton insisted upon giving them a farewell party, she would take no denial, saying that if Everard did not come, that she would not believe that he forgave her."

Grace and Emily were delighted, saying, it was the very thing, and Alice was half wild with glee at being included in the invitation, and also allowed to go.

So Isabel had a new white dress for the occasion, and now that she was no longer the governess, she arrayed herself with some of the beautiful and costly jewels, which her fathers creditors had refused to take, (though they were offered them by Isabel,) which had not seen the light since she came to Elm Grove.

"Oh Isabel, now you look like yourself" said Lucy, who had arrived just in time to be of the party.

"How sly of you Isabel, not to let us see them before" cried Emily examining them "what beauties," and Mrs. Arlington looked very approvingly at her future daughter-in-law. "I think that you are the proudest girl I ever saw, Isabel," she said reproachfully.

"Oh mamma, not proud, only sensitive," interposed Alice warmly.

"I think you were wrong my dear" continued Mrs. Arlington without heeding Alice.

"Please don't', pleaded Isabel the tears gathering in her eyes "I could not help feeling so, indeed I could not."

"Don't blame her mamma, it does not matter now," put in Emily.

"She was a stupid little goose to care so much about it; and I always said so," chimed in Lucy.

"Pray who is a stupid little goose," asked Everard joining the group in the drawing-room.

"Ask no questions—you know the rest" returned Lucy saucily.

"Dear me, how late we shall be" cried Emily "what can make papa and Harry so long."

"On arriving at the Park, an unexpected pleasure caused a great deal of excitement. On entering the dressing-room they met Ada. "Oh, when did you come." I'm so glad." "How delightful." Burst from them simultaneously, as Ada was hugged in a manner that bid fair to ruin the effect of her careful toilet.

"Didn't Lucy tell you," asked Ada amazed.

"Not I," cried Lucy triumphantly.

"Oh Lucy."

Then a thundering rap at the door from Harry, who was impatient to see his sister; made them hasten down, all in high spirits at the unlooked for meeting.

Lady Ashton hardly seemed herself she was so pleasant, and even Grace did the agreeable to perfection.

Lucy, lectured Everard, and condemned severely his taking Isabel to be eaten up by savages; as she persisted would be the case if he carried out his preposterous intentions. But Everard only laughed. "I cannot see how you can reconcile it to your conscience, to doom such a girl as that, to so wretched an existence, look at her, is she fit for such a hum-drum-knock-about life."

"Everard cast a very admiring glance at his bride elect, but his only answer was a rather sad smile.

"Oh I see I am right," she cried, "I know you think that she is more fitted for civilized society, confess now, confess, I used to think you so considerate, but now I see you are very selfish.

"Perhaps I am," and he walked out on the lawn, leaving Lucy much astonished and very indignant.

"Be merciful Lucy," said Charles offering his arm.

"Not I," returned Lucy, "I think it awfully cool."

"Then it must be very refreshing this hot evening" said Charles laughing.

"Don't be provoking." I'm awfully angry."

"Lucy!"

"Charles!"

CHAPTER XXXIV

"Oh, here you are," said Lucy when shortly after breakfast next morning she found Everard enjoying a cigar in the piazza. "You needn't think to escape by going off in that unceremonious manner last night, so you may as well listen now, for I intend to express my sentiments some time or other."

"I am all attention Miss Lucy, only I hope you don't object to my cigar."

"Not at all, it will make you more patient perhaps."

"Shouldn't wonder, as I'm afraid from your preamble it is nothing I care to hear."

"Everard!" then with a shrug. "Of course you don't."

Everard laughed. "You stupid fellow, won't you be quiet and hear what I have to say."

"Oh certainly."

"I wish to remind you, that you need not go goodness knows how many hundred miles to find people to convert, as there are plenty nearer home."

"No doubt, and also, others near home anxious to convert them."

"And do you think, that no one but yourself would go to that outlandish place."

"Very few, comparatively; of course there are some."

"Mighty few I expect."

"Then you see an additional reason, why I should."

"I have not seen any yet, so of course cant't see additional ones" she answered saucily. "I tell you what you had better do, stay and convert me, and that will take you a precious long time I promise you."

"Lucy!"

"Oh, how grave you are, I wish you could see your face."

"You forget what you are talking about, Lucy, or you would not speak so" he said gravely, "I cannot believe that you are in earnest."

"Of course I don't mean half I say, I never do, I did not think you would take it so seriously."

"It is a bad way to get into, Lucy."

"Don't be alarmed" cried Lucy laughing, "I'm not so awfully wicked as you imagine. I know, that I am very wild, and thoughtless, and that that school did not do me any good, but for all that, I'm not quite a heathen."

"Be merry and wise," he said kindly but gravely."

"That is not so easy" returned Lucy with a gulp, "you may think so, you are so mild tempered; but with one, so impulsive, and high spirited as I am, it is very hard, almost impossible; that's always the way with you quiet, easy going people, you have no sympathy with us."

"Oh, Lucy, how apt we are to form wrong opinions, you think me quiet, easy, gentle, I may be so, but I am also passionate, determined, and you say selfish; be that as it may, I cannot give up without a very hard struggle, not even then usually. I am unyielding. Persevering and firm, Emily would say, self-willed and obstinate, Grace would call me."

"I can't believe you."

"It is true."

"But to resume our discussion; it is really too provoking to take Isabel off to that outlandish place."

"It is settled, all the talking in the world can't make any difference," he said with the quiet smile, and languid manner, that made it so hard to believe that he was indeed what he had described.

In the evening Susan brought a note to Isabel, as she and Everard were walking on the terrace. Isabel turned deadly pale on observing the handwriting, "it is from Dr. Tachereau" she exclaimed.

"Let me open it" said Everard seeing her agitation.

"A poisoned letter perhaps."

"Oh Everard, such things only happen in story books, but if you really think so, it had better go at the back of the fire."

"The fire is the right place for it no doubt, but I have a curiosity to see the inside first, some impertinence you may be sure."

"Perhaps to inform us, that he will bring his pistols to the church, if we dare to venture there, said Isabel breaking the seal. She opened it, but a sickening faintness overpowered her, and she was unable to read. He had now succeeded in making her fear him, while his vindictiveness had been solely against herself, she had defied him, but now, that another was menaced she trembled for his safety.

"Let me see this madman's effusion" said Everard soothingly, "Why I declare you are quite ill, take this seat and I will read for our mutual edification."

Casting an anxious glance towards Isabel occasionally to ascertain if she was recovering from her agitation, he read a follow's:

DEAR ISABEL,—(cool muttered Everard). What a fool I was the other night, can you, will you, forgive me. Could you know the remorse and misery I have suffered since, or the feeling of thankfulness with which I heard that I had not seriously injured either of you; I think you would. What a reward for your kindness to my poor Natalie; what a return for your sympathy in my trouble. When had you rejoiced at my misfortune, I could scarcely have been surprised. But I loved myself, and my own way, and you thwarted me twice; but enough of the past. I dare not contemplate it. Let me however say a few words in extenuation of my folly. You can never know what I endured that evening, to see the regard once bestowed on me, transferred to another, to see that I was nothing,—that I was entirely, unmistakeably forgotten,—perhaps detested; for you treated me with unnecessary coldness.

All this so worked upon my unhappy temperament until nearly mad with anger and jealousy, I did that, for which I now beseech you to forgive me. I shall never see you again, as the thought of your marrying another is so hateful to me that I dare not trust myself in your presence after the dark glimpse I have had of my evil nature. I did not think I could be so wicked. Farewell, I still remain your loving, though now unloved—LOUIS.

Everard deliberately tore the note into fragments, with the same expression that Dr. Heathfield had remarked, while an angry flush suffused his countenance. But there was more of pity, than of anger, in Isabel's mind, and she did not notice his displeasure. And as Rose at this moment came to call them in, to see Mrs. Arnold, of course no comment was passed on the letter; though Everard's unusual gloominess that evening, proved that he had not forgotten it.

Mrs. Arnold was very fussy as usual, and told many amusing anecdotes regarding her journey, and also gave an immense amount of good advice to both Everard and Isabel, for which of course they were duly grateful.

"Really my dear Mabel" said Mrs. Arnold, "I never was more glad in my life, than when I heard of this match, I was positively delighted. But you must not suppose for a moment, that I had any such idea; when I got her the situation."

Isabel looked annoyed, "naughty girl" said Mrs. Arlington, and then it came out, how foolishly sensitive, (as Mrs. Arlington termed it,) Isabel had always been, regarding her position. "Never mind, dear," said Mrs. Arnold kindly, "It is all over now, but still I should have thought that you had been a governess long enough to get used to it."

"Please don't pleaded Isabel, resolutely forcing back the tears which invariably came, at any allusion to the distasteful subject. And Everard, who until now had been unaware of her extreme dislike of being a governess admired her the more, that while hating her position so much, she had so determinately refused him, as long as she felt, that she did not return his affection.

"How is it my dear" inquired Mrs. Arnold, who seemed destined to-night to hit upon the wrong topic, "that you have never been to visit any of your old friends, Mrs. Price, Mrs. Vernon, Miss Carding, and hosts of others, told me repeatedly, that time after time, they have sent you the most pressing invitations, all to no purpose."

Isabel reddened painfully, Emily and Lucy laughed.

"That is another of Isabel's 'weaknesses'." Everard looked annoyed. "Sing some of your comic songs, Harry," he said, wishing to change the subject. And Harry sung, to the great amusement of the party generally, and of Mrs. Arnold in particular.

Before they separated, a moonlight excursion to the romantic dell, the scene of the memorable picnic four years ago, was arranged for the next evening, and met with universal approbation. All agreeing that the water-fall could only be seen to perfection by moonlight.

CHAPTER XXXV

It had been a dull day, this last day, so that all were glad that the evening was not spent quietly at home, giving time for sad thoughts of to-morrow's parting. Thanks to Harry and Lucy, the excursion passed off more cheerfully than might have been expected, all appearing to enjoy themselves. On their return, Isabel did not join the others in the drawing-room, but went out and lingered by the fountain, in the moonlight, musing on all that had happened since she first came there, now nearly five years ago, and wondering how long it might be, and what might happen, ere she would again be there—or if, indeed, she would be there again. Ah! seek not to look into futurity, Isabel. It is well for you that you know not all that shall be ere you again sit there. Enjoy your happiness while you may, and leave the future to unfold itself. She remained there a long time thinking of many things, and was still lost in meditation when Everard joined her.

"A penny for your thoughts," he said.

"Oh, Everard, I want you to do something," she returned, laying her hand on his arm.

"What is it, dearest?" he inquired.

"I feel so unhappy about Louis. I wish so much that you would write and say that we forgive him."

Everard was silent, and his face became very stern.

"If you would, I should be so glad."

"You ask too much," he said.

"Only what is right."

"Right perhaps, but hard—very hard."

"Oh, do," she pleaded, raising her blue eyes to his so earnestly. "Oh, Everard, it is not the way for us to be happy, to be unforgiving. I should be so miserable: day by day watching the blue waters, knowing that I had left any one in anger or ill-feeling. Oh, Everard, you will forgive him!"

She looked so lovely there in the moonlight, pleading for one who so little deserved it of her, that Everard found it hard to refuse her.

"I cannot write a lie, Isabel, even to please you," he replied, in a harsh, unnatural voice.

"Oh, no, not that; but I want you really to forgive him."

"I do not, I cannot," and his voice was hard and cold.

Isabel shuddered. Was this the Everard usually so kind and gentle?

"Oh, Everard, and you a clergyman!"

"Perhaps I am not fit to be one," he answered. "I have

thought so sometimes lately, but I wished so much to be one that, in seeking to fulfil the wish, I may have overlooked the meetness."

"If you are not, I do not know who is," she said, "but this is not like yourself; I should be less surprised if I was unforgiving and you forgave."

"I hope that I do not often feel as I do now towards him. But you forget how nearly he took you from me; he whom I trusted and regarded with the warmest friendship."

"It is not for his sake I ask it Everard; forgive as you would be forgiven."

They walked on in silence until they reached the house. Then Everard said, "From my heart I wish I could, Isabel," and abruptly left her. Then, alone in his own room, after all had retired to rest, far into the night he fought the battle of good and evil. What was he about to do—preach and teach meekness, self-denial, and forgiveness of injuries, while he was still angry and unforgiving? What mockery! Ought he not to practice what he taught? Was theory—mere words—sufficient? No; he must, by example, give force to his teaching, or how could he hope to succeed? All this he saw clearly enough, but the difficulty still remained. He strove hard to conquer, but evil prevailed. "Forgive as you would be forgiven" rang continually in his ears, but he did not, could not, forgive. He laid down, but not to sleep, and the pale moon shone calmly and peacefully in upon him, as if mocking his disquietude. At length he threw the painful subject from him, and sank into an uneasy slumber.

He awoke, next morning, with the sun beaming brightly in at the window. But dark clouds gathered round him; gloomy doubts as to his fitness for the office he had taken, and

Clotilda Jennings

sorrow at the impossibility of his forgiving Louis. "Forgive as you would be forgiven," and again the last night's struggle was renewed, and even when they started for the church he had not conquered.

Isabel saw how it was, and this was the bitter drop in her cup of happiness. Alas! in this world when is it unalloyed?

A burst of music filled the church as the bridal party entered, and very lovely looked the bride, surrounded by her three little bridesmaids, while in the background stood a fourth, the merry Lucy. Bob and three youthful Arlington cousins were groomsmen, and Everard, to use Lucy's own words, was the very *beau ideal* of what a bridegroom should be, in fact "perfect."

The sun shone with almost dazzling splendor on the group, which Emily pronounced "a good omen," and again the organ pealed forth its joyous strains as they left the church, and gaily rang the marriage bells.

"Everard," said Isabel, when they were in the library awaiting the arrival of the others, "write that letter now; I know you can, for you would not look so happy if you felt as you did last night."

"I can write it truthfully now," he replied, smiling at her earnestness. And then, with his bride bending over his shoulder, Everard wrote such a note as only *he* could write, expressing their entire forgiveness, and made Isabel take the pen and write "Isabel Arlington" under his signature.

The others, coming in, insisted upon knowing the subject of their very important correspondence, but Everard pocketed the letter and refused to satisfy their curiosity.

The breakfast was but a dull affair, notwithstanding the exuberant spirits of the young groomsmen. The parents knew that they were parting with their only son, and that it would be years before they would see him again; and the son, amid his happiness, remembered that he was leaving father, mother, sisters, perhaps never to return. Isabel, also, felt it hard to part so soon with her new sisters, who hung about her with every demonstration of affection and regret.

Then such a scene in the dressing-room (from which Mrs. Arlington had mercifully contrived to keep Mrs. Arnold.) Emily, with her head buried in a sofa cushion, weeping passionately at the thought of parting with her brother, while the children all clung around Isabel in such a manner as to make it utterly impossible for her to don her travelling dress; Lucy trying to comfort Emily, and Grace scolding the children. Ada, taking pity on Isabel, reminded them that Everard was going as well as Isabel, suggesting that they should go down to him. To this they readily agreed.

"I ought to go, too, only I'm afraid Everard will be vexed to see me in such a state," sobbed Emily.

"I like to have you here, Emily dear," replied Isabel, "but you had better go down; you will be sorry afterwards if you don't. He feels it dreadfully, I know, poor fellow."

"He looked fearfully pale during breakfast," added Ada, feelingly.

"I will go," returned Emily, vainly endeavoring to check her emotion. And Grace went with her, leaving Isabel with Ada and Lucy.

Isabel, who had managed to keep up tolerably well so far, now gave way to uncontrollable emotion. This second scene with the children had been quite too much for her.

"Isabel! Isabel! you will never be dressed to-day," cried Ada, in despair.

"Oh, let her be," returned Lucy; "they will miss the train, and have to wait for the next steamer. What a glorious stew Everard would be in! for then, of course, they would be too late for that precious Indian ship. Oh, I declare, I hope they will!"

"Oh, Lucy!" and Isabel made quick work with her dressing, to Lucy's intense amusement.

Everard, meanwhile, had been undergoing a terrible ordeal down stairs, and was truly glad when Isabel made her appearance. She was met now with a worse storm of grief than any previously encountered; as for Amy, she flew into the carriage after her.

So they drove off, amid thundering cheers from the young groomsmen. Papa inquired if Amy intended to go to Madagascar, and on Everard's answering in the affirmative she was wild to get out, protesting that she would not. "But you can't get out until we reach the gate," said Everard. "Promise me, Isabel, dear Isabel, that you will let me out at the gate," she cried, in an agony; "pray don't let me go to nasty Madagascar; oh, please don't." So Everard, seeing that the child was really terrified, stopped the carriage, and Amy instantly jumped out in the greatest haste, without waiting for any more leave-taking, getting several thumps from the old shoes which were sent in a continued shower after the carriage until it had passed through the gate, when a deafening "tiger" made the welkin ring.

* * * * * * * *

Here we must bid adieu to those whose fortunes we have followed so far, hoping at some future time to hear more about them. But as we do not care to inquire particularly after Louis Taschereau, we may as well mention here that he, some time after, married a fine high-spirited girl, who was completely his match, the domineering being all on the wife's side. No tears were shed by her during his absence, and a scornful smile was the utmost that his anger or ill-temper ever elicited. So they managed to get on tolerably well, the inquiring look of the cold grey eye often checking a fit of passion. As Louis's mercenary propensities have already shown themselves, it is almost needless to add that she had what he valued more than anything else—money—which, by the way, she took good care to have settled on herself. But this he did not object to (albeit she would have done so all the same if he had), provided there was plenty of it.

Choose from Thousands of 1stWorldLibrary Classics By

A. M. Barnard
Ada Leverson
Adolphus William Ward
Aesop
Agatha Christie
Alexander Aaronsohn
Alexander Kielland
Alexandre Dumas
Alfred Gatty
Alfred Ollivant
Alice Duer Miller
Alice Turner Curtis
Alice Dunbar
Allen Chapman
Alleyne Ireland
Ambrose Bierce
Amelia E. Barr
Amory H. Bradford
Andrew Lang
Andrew McFarland Davis
Andy Adams
Angela Brazil
Anna Alice Chapin
Anna Sewell
Annie Besant
Annie Hamilton Donnell
Annie Payson Call
Annie Roe Carr
Annonaymous
Anton Chekhov
Archibald Lee Fletcher
Arnold Bennett
Arthur C. Benson
Arthur Conan Doyle
Arthur M. Winfield
Arthur Ransome
Arthur Schnitzler
Arthur Train
Atticus
B.H. Baden-Powell
B. M. Bower
B. C. Chatterjee
Baroness Emmuska Orczy
Baroness Orczy
Basil King
Bayard Taylor
Ben Macomber
Bertha Muzzy Bower
Bjornstjerne Bjornson

Booth Tarkington
Boyd Cable
Bram Stoker
C. Collodi
C. E. Orr
C. M. Ingleby
Carolyn Wells
Catherine Parr Traill
Charles A. Eastman
Charles Amory Beach
Charles Dickens
Charles Dudley Warner
Charles Farrar Browne
Charles Ives
Charles Kingsley
Charles Klein
Charles Hanson Towne
Charles Lathrop Pack
Charles Romyn Dake
Charles Whibley
Charles Willing Beale
Charlotte M. Braeme
Charlotte M. Yonge
Charlotte Perkins Stetson
Clair W. Hayes
Clarence Day Jr.
Clarence E. Mulford
Clemence Housman
Confucius
Coningsby Dawson
Cornelis DeWitt Wilcox
Cyril Burleigh
D. H. Lawrence
Daniel Defoe
David Garnett
Dinah Craik
Don Carlos Janes
Donald Keyhoe
Dorothy Kilner
Dougan Clark
Douglas Fairbanks
E. Nesbit
E. P. Roe
E. Phillips Oppenheim
E. S. Brooks
Earl Barnes
Edgar Rice Burroughs
Edith Van Dyne
Edith Wharton

Edward Everett Hale
Edward J. O'Biren
Edward S. Ellis
Edwin L. Arnold
Eleanor Atkins
Eleanor Hallowell Abbott
Eliot Gregory
Elizabeth Gaskell
Elizabeth McCracken
Elizabeth Von Arnim
Ellem Key
Emerson Hough
Emilie F. Carlen
Emily Bronte
Emily Dickinson
Enid Bagnold
Enilor Macartney Lane
Erasmus W. Jones
Ernie Howard Pie
Ethel May Dell
Ethel Turner
Ethel Watts Mumford
Eugene Sue
Eugenie Foa
Eugene Wood
Eustace Hale Ball
Evelyn Everett-green
Everard Cotes
F. H. Cheley
F. J. Cross
F. Marion Crawford
Fannie E. Newberry
Federick Austin Ogg
Ferdinand Ossendowski
Fergus Hume
Florence A. Kilpatrick
Fremont B. Deering
Francis Bacon
Francis Darwin
Frances Hodgson Burnett
Frances Parkinson Keyes
Frank Gee Patchin
Frank Harris
Frank Jewett Mather
Frank L. Packard
Frank V. Webster
Frederic Stewart Isham
Frederick Trevor Hill
Frederick Winslow Taylor

Friedrich Kerst
Friedrich Nietzsche
Fyodor Dostoyevsky
G.A. Henty
G.K. Chesterton
Gabrielle E. Jackson
Garrett P. Serviss
Gaston Leroux
George A. Warren
George Ade
Geroge Bernard Shaw
George Cary Eggleston
George Durston
George Ebers
George Eliot
George Gissing
George MacDonald
George Meredith
George Orwell
George Sylvester Viereck
George Tucker
George W. Cable
George Wharton James
Gertrude Atherton
Gordon Casserly
Grace E. King
Grace Gallatin
Grace Greenwood
Grant Allen
Guillermo A. Sherwell
Gulielma Zollinger
Gustav Flaubert
H. A. Cody
H. B. Irving
H.C. Bailey
H. G. Wells
H. H. Munro
H. Irving Hancock
H. R. Naylor
H. Rider Haggard
H. W. C. Davis
Haldeman Julius
Hall Caine
Hamilton Wright Mabie
Hans Christian Andersen
Harold Avery
Harold McGrath
Harriet Beecher Stowe
Harry Castlemon
Harry Coghill
Harry Houidini

Hayden Carruth
Helent Hunt Jackson
Helen Nicolay
Hendrik Conscience
Hendy David Thoreau
Henri Barbusse
Henrik Ibsen
Henry Adams
Henry Ford
Henry Frost
Henry James
Henry Jones Ford
Henry Seton Merriman
Henry W Longfellow
Herbert A. Giles
Herbert Carter
Herbert N. Casson
Herman Hesse
Hildegard G. Frey
Homer
Honore De Balzac
Horace B. Day
Horace Walpole
Horatio Alger Jr.
Howard Pyle
Howard R. Garis
Hugh Lofting
Hugh Walpole
Humphry Ward
Ian Maclaren
Inez Haynes Gillmore
Irving Bacheller
Isabel Cecilia Williams
Isabel Hornibrook
Israel Abrahams
Ivan Turgenev
J.G.Austin
J. Henri Fabre
J. M. Barrie
J. M. Walsh
J. Macdonald Oxley
J. R. Miller
J. S. Fletcher
J. S. Knowles
J. Storer Clouston
J. W. Duffield
Jack London
Jacob Abbott
James Allen
James Andrews
James Baldwin

James Branch Cabell
James DeMille
James Joyce
James Lane Allen
James Lane Allen
James Oliver Curwood
James Oppenheim
James Otis
James R. Driscoll
Jane Abbott
Jane Austen
Jane L. Stewart
Janet Aldridge
Jens Peter Jacobsen
Jerome K. Jerome
Jessie Graham Flower
John Buchan
John Burroughs
John Cournos
John F. Kennedy
John Gay
John Glasworthy
John Habberton
John Joy Bell
John Kendrick Bangs
John Milton
John Philip Sousa
John Taintor Foote
Jonas Lauritz Idemil Lie
Jonathan Swift
Joseph A. Altsheler
Joseph Carey
Joseph Conrad
Joseph E. Badger Jr
Joseph Hergesheimer
Joseph Jacobs
Jules Vernes
Julian Hawthrone
Julie A Lippmann
Justin Huntly McCarthy
Kakuzo Okakura
Karle Wilson Baker
Kate Chopin
Kenneth Grahame
Kenneth McGaffey
Kate Langley Bosher
Kate Langley Bosher
Katherine Cecil Thurston
Katherine Stokes
L. A. Abbot
L. T. Meade

L. Frank Baum
Latta Griswold
Laura Dent Crane
Laura Lee Hope
Laurence Housman
Lawrence Beasley
Leo Tolstoy
Leonid Andreyev
Lewis Carroll
Lewis Sperry Chafer
Lilian Bell
Lloyd Osbourne
Louis Hughes
Louis Joseph Vance
Louis Tracy
Louisa May Alcott
Lucy Fitch Perkins
Lucy Maud Montgomery
Luther Benson
Lydia Miller Middleton
Lyndon Orr
M. Corvus
M. H. Adams
Margaret E. Sangster
Margret Howth
Margaret Vandercook
Margaret W. Hungerford
Margret Penrose
Maria Edgeworth
Maria Thompson Daviess
Mariano Azuela
Marion Polk Angellotti
Mark Overton
Mark Twain
Mary Austin
Mary Catherine Crowley
Mary Cole
Mary Hastings Bradley
Mary Roberts Rinehart
Mary Rowlandson
M. Wollstonecraft Shelley
Maud Lindsay
Max Beerbohm
Myra Kelly
Nathaniel Hawthrone
Nicolo Machiavelli
O. F. Walton
Oscar Wilde

Owen Johnson
P.G. Wodehouse
Paul and Mabel Thorne
Paul G. Tomlinson
Paul Severing
Percy Brebner
Percy Keese Fitzhugh
Peter B. Kyne
Plato
Quincy Allen
R. Derby Holmes
R. L. Stevenson
R. S. Ball
Rabindranath Tagore
Rahul Alvares
Ralph Bonehill
Ralph Henry Barbour
Ralph Victor
Ralph Waldo Emmerson
Rene Descartes
Ray Cummings
Rex Beach
Rex E. Beach
Richard Harding Davis
Richard Jefferies
Richard Le Gallienne
Robert Barr
Robert Frost
Robert Gordon Anderson
Robert L. Drake
Robert Lansing
Robert Lynd
Robert Michael Ballantyne
Robert W. Chambers
Rosa Nouchette Carey
Rudyard Kipling
Saint Augustine
Samuel B. Allison
Samuel Hopkins Adams
Sarah Bernhardt
Sarah C. Hallowell
Selma Lagerlof
Sherwood Anderson
Sigmund Freud
Standish O'Grady
Stanley Weyman
Stella Benson
Stella M. Francis

Stephen Crane
Stewart Edward White
Stijn Streuvels
Swami Abhedananda
Swami Parmananda
T. S. Ackland
T. S. Arthur
The Princess Der Ling
Thomas A. Janvier
Thomas A Kempis
Thomas Anderton
Thomas Bailey Aldrich
Thomas Bulfinch
Thomas De Quincey
Thomas Dixon
Thomas H. Huxley
Thomas Hardy
Thomas More
Thornton W. Burgess
U. S. Grant
Upton Sinclair
Valentine Williams
Various Authors
Vaughan Kester
Victor Appleton
Victor G. Durham
Victoria Cross
Virginia Woolf
Wadsworth Camp
Walter Camp
Walter Scott
Washington Irving
Wilbur Lawton
Wilkie Collins
Willa Cather
Willard F. Baker
William Dean Howells
William le Queux
W. Makepeace Thackeray
William W. Walter
William Shakespeare
Winston Churchill
Yei Theodora Ozaki
Yogi Ramacharaka
Young E. Allison
Zane Grey